Situationz 2

by
D'Vine Pen

ISBN: 978-1-7343587-1-1

Situationz 2

Copyright © 2020 by Dela Morgan

For permission requests, please contact the author via email at divinepenent@gmail.com

Proudly self-published through Divine Legacy Publishing, www.divinelegacypublishing.com

Dedication

This book is dedicated to my friend Carmen Hendrix.

Thank you for being an amazing sister/friend and publisher. I'm using the tools that you taught me to continue my legacy, which I know you're proud of. I'm continuing what we started, so there is no way to go but up.

God gained an angel and you are truly missed.

Rest well my friend.

Acknowledgements

Thank you to Amanda Chambers and Divine Legacy Publishing. You are an amazing publisher. I appreciate the fact that you saw my vision and you never let me give up. We spent many late nights getting great work accomplished. I appreciate you more than you'll ever know Sis.

Thank you to my daughter Jasmine. My mini me. You kept me going and I do all of this for you. You are my legacy and my light!

Thank you to every fan of the series. I loved every book club I've been asked to attend, every interview and enjoyed every question. Hearing your responses to Situationz clarified that this had to be a series because we are just starting with JaNae, Bri and Denise. They have so much more in store. These Situations are 2 hot 2 handle.

Smooches~

D'Vine Pen

Chapter 1
JaNae

Location: The Hotel Hilton Americas in the heart of downtown Houston Texas.

The theme was An Elegant Evening in Autumn.

The ballroom accommodated 200 guests. It included an 18-foot draped ceiling. Dim lighting bounced off glimmering custom chandeliers, creating an enchanted ambiance and giving the room a dose of glamor. Hand strung Swarovski crystal garlands draped throughout the walls. Tables displayed lavish center pieces, flowers, and lighting in and array of reds, burnt orange, and browns, which gave a warm fuzzy feeling of drinking hot chocolate with the one you love in front of a crackling fireplace.

On this day, October 1st, guests were in awe of the beautiful venue, designed to celebrate the union of Mr. and Mrs. Chase Reynolds. Planning this wedding was not only important to me because Brianna and Chase are high profile clients and it was amazing for my brand, but because they were family. Brianna was my best friend and she was marrying the love of her life Chase, who had become a brother to me. Bri was happy and in love, and it looked damn good on her. One day I hoped to find my Boaz as well.

Denise and I equally shared Maid of Honor titles. Denise was the completion to this best friend trio. We used every resource we had to make sure Bri didn't have to lift a finger, especially since she just got off of a three-month world tour as head choreographer for multiple artists. To say that Denise's parents have long money was an understatement. Her mother also had ties with many of the elite in Houston that wouldn't want to piss her off. If it wasn't for Denise, I would have pulled my hair out a long time ago. I was such a perfectionist. Whatever my client wanted, they got, or as long as it fit into their budget. My bestie was lucky I love her to death because my services don't run cheap, but for my girls I would do pretty much anything.

It was now time for the show to begin. Pastor Leavy, Chase, and his best man Michael walked into the room from the right side door entrance to take their places at the altar. Most men looked nervous on a day like today. Not Chase. He was cool and calm awaiting his queen. On cue, our line sister Shana started to sing "A Couple of Forevers" by Chrisette Michele. This was the signal to all of the wedding party that it was our time to shine. Of course, I micromanaged every possible detail that I could until I was forced to hand over my walkie to my assistant Amber. See what I mean by protectionist? Everything flowed and was going according to plan.

Sean Thomas Bridal Couture designed the gowns for the wedding party. The bridesmaids wore plum colored long one-shoulder, crinkle chiffon dresses with a thigh high split and a cinched waist. Nude 5-inch stiletto pumps and gold tear drop earrings accompanied this look. Chase preferred to take care of the groomsmen with his personal tailor. Once I saw the picture of the tuxedo that was selected, I was satisfied but to see this handsome line of men before me was a different beast. I must say, they all cleaned up rather nicely.

The ladies held bouquets arranged with orchids, tiger lilies, and roses. Each groomsman took a bridesmaids hand, then walked them down the aisle. Each couple was stopped for a few photos then continued to the altar where they separated from their partners for the ceremony. Jada, Bri's sister, walked down the aisle by herself because she was the Matron of Honor. Michael would accompany her once the ceremony was finished. All six bridesmaids and groomsmen were in place. My daughter Angel and Chase's nephew Lance came down the aisle together, our flower girl and ring bearer. They were just so cute. Awwww's erupted from the crowd as the two of them made their way down the aisle waving and speaking to everyone and practically stealing the show. I winked at my baby to let her know she did a great job as I stood holding my bouquet awaiting the bride.

200 guests stood to their feet as the doors opened to reveal a magnificent sight. Brianna stood at the entrance with her father waiting to grace us with her presence. Draped over her perfectly toned body was a custom-made dream: A sheer and cream sweetheart neckline, long sleeve mermaid wedding gown that was embellished in gold. Her crystal peek toe Jimmy Choo's had her standing tall with confidence. Bri looked stunning as she got closer and closer to her future.

I could hear Chase say, "Damn!"

Glad we aren't in a church, I thought.

Her father pulled her veil over her head, kissed her on the cheek, and told his oldest daughter how much he loved her. He beamed with pride as he handed her off to her husband to be.

Smiling he whispered to Chase, "Keep her happy, or I'm gone come looking for you!" The few that heard him had a chuckle at Chase's expense.

"Who gives this woman away?" Pastor Leary asked.

"We do," Bri's parents stated in unison.

"You may be seated," Pastor Leary's commanded.

Bri passed her embellished and beaded bouquet to Daja so she could now confess her love. As vows were exchanged, the nostalgic feelings of love overflowed throughout the room. There was no way you weren't going to be touched. Quiet tears were shed at the blessed and joyful occasion. I personally had been too busy with Angel and my career to notice something was missing.

"Girl, are you okay?" Denise whispered to me.

"I guess I never noticed what I was missing out on until now," I told her.

"Sis, it's time to finally let someone in. Your happiness is out there, but you have to be willing to be happy," she told me.

"You may now kiss the bride!" I hear Pastor Leary say as the room erupted in cheers for the happy couple.

I was in my own head and missed out on part of the ceremony. *Pull it together Nae,* I told myself.

The bride and groom exited the alter, and one by one each couple in the bridal party followed suit. It was time for the cocktail hour as the room was transformed for the reception. Time to check with my team to make sure things were running smoothly. Look at me, always on the job. These people were well trained and fully capable of taking care of business. Hell, it was time for me to have fun.

Cocktail hour had an array of hors d'oeuvres to snack on while waiting for the reception to begin in 20 minutes. The bridal party grabbed something quick and then we were rushed off to take pictures.

"I want to say something. Nae, this day has been way more than I ever could have imagined and I love it. Your vision for my dream wedding went above and beyond. Having everyone who is near and dear to my heart makes this day even better. We love you all! Thank you for being my circle." Bri shed a few tears as she addressed Denise, Daja and, myself.

"Sis, enough of that because there is no place we would rather be. Let's raise our glasses to the happy couple. Glasses up," Daja said and we all raised our glasses in unison to toast the happy couple.

It was nice to sit back and have fun. I hadn't laughed this hard and let my hair down in a long time. Everything was work, work, work. Just being here with my girls was something I needed more often. These were the best years of our lives, and I needed to do more living in mine.

The night was a success and everything came together the way it should. In true Psi Kappa Psi fashion, we couldn't let the night pass without letting the bride lead the way as we strolled for all of the guests to see. Bri was cutting loose like we were in college again. Thank goodness the dress for the reception was short, which gave her the ability to move like she wanted.

While we were on the dance floor strolling with our Soros, out of my peripheral vision I saw someone coming toward us. I looked to my left in the direction of the figure approaching, and I couldn't believe my eyes. I knew I had a few drinks, but were my eyes deceiving me? Heading towards me with suaveness like none I had still yet to see, James appeared before me. He wore a blue pin striped tailor made suit and clean dark brown shoes.

The music slowed down, and he took me into his arms without warning and held me close. I was doing everything in my power not to melt. Lord this man still had that effect on me after all of these years. My head naturally laid on his shoulder, and I took in his sweet masculine smells. Lord have Mercy on me now. It was probably a puddle around my feet with the way this man was instantly turning me on. I knew I was wrong for pushing him away after my mother's death.

"It's good seeing you Ma. I've been laying low in the background waiting to talk to you." His east coast twang was one I missed.

"James, I'm sorry about how I acted . . ." I tried to say but was stopped.

"That's old. I understand, and we are here now. I just moved back to Texas a month ago. I knew it was a chance that I would see you, so I made it my business to be here," he told me.

"All of these years, I thought you hated me. I heard you moved back to Jersey, so assumed I would never see you again," I confessed.

"We obviously have a lot of catching up to do." James planted an innocent kiss on my neck that sent chills up my spine.

"Mommy Mommy Mommy!" Angel said stepping between us.

"Mommy?" James asked, a look of surprise clear on his face.

Chapter 2
James

When Chase told me he was making it official with his queen, my first thought was "I'm there." The next thought that invaded my mind was the possibility of seeing HER again. So long ago we were about to start something that neither one of us could deny. Unfortunately, tragedy derailed our plans. JaNae wore the world on her shoulders once her mother passed away. I tried my best to be there for her, but my efforts fell on deaf ears, forcing me to fall back. I can't lie; this isn't something I'm used to when it comes to women. She was the first woman to challenge me and make me feel something more than numb at the thought of relationships. To this day, the thought of her has a certain effect on me.

Prior to graduating college, I gained knowledge of business and an open mind from several internships, which led to multiple offers once I achieved my degree. The one that peeked my interest the most was an urban clothing company in New York. Living down south was a beautiful thing, but I felt I needed the grit of the East Coast under my feet. Who would have known that working in fashion would have changed my way of thinking in general? I was more of a jeans and t-shirt type of guy, but my whole style was outlawed at work. Every day you had to dress for success. No jeans or baggy clothes, Timbs or tennis shoes. It was not just changing a style of clothing but a frame of mind. When you looked like success, you were bound to be successful was the motto behind the dress code. Slowly but surely, I saw a change in myself. I got with the program and learned everything possible on a business aspect as well as design. I took that knowledge and started my own business wear line called Confirm, for the professional man including suits, tuxedos, shirts, slacks, shoes and accessories. Confirm was a clothing line that fits any style of man.

Swag and confidence are important on a man, but a man that can wear a nice suit with commas in the bank is way more attractive.

My clothing line was what brought me back to Texas. My line has was dominating in men's markets throughout the eastern region, so now it was time to bring it down south. Sagging jeans and snap backs were a thing of the past. If you're out here making money you need to look the part. So bruh, I got you.

My wedding gift to Chase was custom fits for the groomsmen. No rentals this way baby. Of course for myself I had to get a little something special made for the big day. I wasn't in the wedding due to the move being so hectic with my business. Fade crisp and beard game was on point. This was a special occasion, but it was also business. I looked at every opportunity as a business opportunity and what better place to showcase my brand than this? Gotta give the people something to talk about.

"Bro, I just wanted to give you a heads up that ya girl is the wedding planner, and she is in the wedding," Chase said, awaiting my reaction.

"My girl huh? I see you got jokes. It will be good to see shorty though, it's been awhile," I told him.

"Man you know you wanna see her ass. Don't hit me with that cool shit." He dapped me up, and we both had to laugh. Chase had been my boy since high school so he knew my true feelings for JaNae.

"Look, I'm gone see where her head is at. That's all I can do. Worse come to worse, we remain friends and catch up," I said. I didn't know if I was trying to convince Chase or myself.

"Hey do what you want, but keeping it all the way 100 with you bro, the both of you need to stop playing finally and get this shit together. You not slick and neither is she. Both of you have been keeping tabs on each other for years through me and Bri. Bro, you never give females that much thought. It's like they have an expiration date or something. All of em except Nae. I know you," Chase advised.

"I got this, don't worry about it."

Now I was helping Chase and the groomsmen prepare at the hotel before the wedding. I had to make sure everything was right to send my boy off with style. We had two photographers scheduled. One was the wedding photographer, and I had my own photographer because these photos would not only be wedding memories but advertisements for the website. The photo that stood out the most placed Chase and I in front of his groomsmen that were spread out in a V shape holding cigars. That was the money shot right there. The way that Chase and I dominated the photos gave me an idea. He could be the face of the new line. Oh yeah, we were discussing this at a later date. Being business minded, my mind worked 1000 miles per minute.

It was time to get the show on the road. Arriving at the venue, I saw guests and well-wishers entering the building. As I headed to the bar for a Hennessy, I saw a sight that took my breath away. I must say she was still beautiful and sexy plus thick in all the right places just like I liked em. JaNae passionately talked into her headset making wedding preparations as she walked around with the caterer. She was running shit and taking names. Before I could finish taking in her beauty, she disappeared into the back. I started to feel that familiar feeling of nervousness that only came when I was with her.

Shortly the wedding began and things moved like a fine oiled machine. You couldn't miss the details in every aspect of the venue. The ceremony was filled with love. I was happy for them both. I could honestly say I saw Chase change into a better man with Bri by his side. Bri and Chase made a beautiful couple. To have a relationship like theirs was timeless.

During the intermission between the wedding and the reception I got a call from a very unpleasant number. My kids mother Lisa. My twins were going on four and to say that their mother and I didn't get along was a true understatement. During an internship while in New York, I met Lisa at a bar around the way. We would hook up from time to time when I was in the city for the summer. Before the end of my last year she told me she was pregnant. That was the main reason I came to New York after college. It wasn't the ideal situation, but I tried to make it work for the sake of my kids. I wanted my children to have a father in the household, which was the opposite of my childhood. J.J. (James Jr) and Jaden were my world, but Lisa lacked maternal instincts. She preferred to run the streets and live the party scene. I wanted a woman to be a mother to my kids and a future wifey to me. That wasn't in her plans, and the constant bullshit got old, therefore we parted ways. Shit really hit the fan when I moved back to Texas. She saw me in a BET article and since then it had been all about child support and court dates. I took care of my kids, and they wanted for nothing, but it was never enough for this chick. Just wanted a nigga by the balls.

"Yes Lisa, how can I help you?" I said, not disguising the fact that I was annoyed by her voice.

"Look I didn't call you, your kids did. You better be a little nicer to me before we end up back in court. Ha!" she taunted. Damn this chic stayed with the BS.

"Yo put my fucking kids on the phone, or I will take yo ass to court for not letting me talk to them! Who you think got time for these games? You playing checkers and trust I'm playing chess." This was the shit that I was talking about. You gotta watch who you lay down with.

"Whateva." Sucking her teeth she reluctantly put my kids on the phone. I talked to my prince then my princess about their week. They held top priority in my life no matter what was going on with me and their moms.

After disconnecting the call, I had a smile on my face which only they provided. Now let's get back to the situation at hand. I chose to sit back and peep the scene. Seeing a genuine smile across JaNae's lips was something I didn't realize I missed so much. I didn't think to find out if this lady had a man or even a woman these days, hell who knows. There was no time like the present.

I startled her ass damn near speechless when she locked her eyes with mine. I pulled her into my arms to let her know it was okay. This was a second chance. Before I could finish my thoughts, the flower girl came over to get her mother's attention. Wow, she has a daughter. That never crossed my mind.

"I guess we have a lot of catching up to do," she told me as I looked at the mini JaNae with gray eyes who had climbed in her arms.

"And who is this little lady?" I asked holding out my hand to shake her tiny hand.

"James, this is Angel. Angel, this is mommy's friend Mr. James."

"Hi Mr. James. Mommy, Mommy look my tooth is loose. The tooth fairy is coming soon." Angel wiggled her tooth and showed her mom.

"Okay baby, I see it. You have to be patient and wait for it to fall out or she won't come. So, go be a good girl," JaNae told her.

"Okay Mommy, I will." Angel kissed her mom on the cheek, and wiggled down, and skipped away.

I could see an extra light about her because of her daughter. I took Nae back into my arms, and we danced the night away and had a good time with our family and friends who were happy to see us in the moment. Throughout the night we talked and exchanged numbers so we could see where things could go from there.

I didn't know what to expect when the day started, but I now knew one thing: second chances were possible.

Chapter 3
Brianna

Dance had been my passion for as long as I could walk. My mom said that as a toddler, whenever music was on, I was always moving. When I was a kid I remember mimicking routines for anyone who would watch. I forced Denise and JaNae to learn them with me so we could kill it at school parties. Dance offered me refuge when I had no one to talk to about becoming a teen mom or my parents divorce. It was my escape from the negatives that life had to offer. Instead of getting high or drunk, my drug of choice was the dance floor. This gave me an outlet to pour out my heart. All I needed to make me happy was four walls and a mirror. In college, I was happy with being a professional dancer for musical performances, stage plays, and individual performers. Eventually I built the courage to step out of my comfort zone to pitch my own choreography. Becoming a lead choreographer put me in the position to create outstanding performances for competitions, movie productions, and also joining the winning team for multiple acts at 2018's Coachella or should I say

Bey-chella. I followed in the footsteps of greats that came before me such as Debbie Allen, Rosie Perez, Fatima Robinson, and Laure Ann Gibson, Ms. Boom Boom Kack herself.

I thanked God for having such an understanding husband. He supported my career even though it could lead me away from home for months at a time. After being away from this succulent man of mine, we decided on something simple for our honeymoon. We chose to have a good time in Miami. We just needed some us time. Laying on the beach gazing out at the blue waters of Miami, home of the baddest bitch Trina.

I continuously reminisced on one of the best days of my life. The day that I said, "I Do". I could not have dreamt of a more outstanding wedding day. It was like a diamond and autumn festival. Other than picking out my wedding gown, all I had to do was show up and be pampered. Daja had a spa day set up for me so I had nothing to stress about, and I was not involved in the hustle and bustle of the wedding details. Nae has taken her event planning to new heights. She started out in communications and did party planning as a hobby. With each event, her game was elevated more than the last. Before you knew it, she was working with the who's who of the southern region. We had our own little David Tutera on our hands. I was so proud of her.

Denise and Daja kicked the wedding festivities off with my bridal shower and bachelorette party. The bridal shower was sweet and elegant and included my mom, my aunties, and other elders in our families. But honey, that bachelorette party was everything! We brought the party to Atlanta. 20 of my closest friends, family, and Sorors flew in to send me off right. The girls arranged male and female strippers and dollars were flying everywhere. Drinks were flowing and we all kicked it for three days straight. You could tell some of them heffas needed to get out more often. Pent up housewives didn't know how to act. Everyone had a good time. Daja had a better time than others. I accidentally walked in on her having a three-way with two of the strippers, one male and one female in the bathroom. Well damn! I was drunk as hell at the time so I just closed the door and kept it moving. All I know is, I had a damn good time and ATL didn't owe me a damn thing!

Today I sat back and watched Chase run on the beach shirtless, which was nothing more than breathtaking. Lord his muscles glistened in the sunlight as the sweat dripped off of his skin. Without knowing it, I licked my lips as my eyes traced the front his body and the muscles that led down to a V shape that introduced you to his manhood, which was my favorite body part. Next to his heart of course. I could only smile as I watched other women's reaction as heads turned about to break their necks to catch a glimpse of this Adonis when he passed them by. Yezzzzzz honey, he was all mine! I was Mrs. Chase Reynolds, put some respek on my name!

Once my baby was done giving everyone an eye full, he laid a nice kiss on my lips and had a seat beside me.

"Baby, I see you sitting over here in that bikini with ya ass all out. Don't make me hurt nobody." Chase playfully smacked me on my nice brown round, thanks to my 50 squats a day challenge I got from Cherri, the best trainer in all of Houston, if you ask me. She was one of Denise's many boo thangs.

"You know I'm saving all of this for daddy," I seductively said licking my lips yet again.

"Girl don't start nothing you can't finish, we can go half on a baby right now!"

"Now that I have finally slowed down with my schedule, there is nothing else I would rather do," I said looking at my future in his eyes.

My husband swooped me up in his arms like it was nothing and we headed back to our room. The amount of PDA that was displayed caused discomfort for hotel guests, but we were in our own little world. This was what newlyweds did. Thank God that we were alone in the elevator because we couldn't keep our hands off one other. Finally making it to our room, we left a trail of clothes from the door to our bed. Chase picked me up, laid me on the bed, and looked deeply into my eyes.

"Once you came into my life I knew you were the woman I was going to marry and start a family with. Babe, you are my everything. You make me a better man," my husband expressed to me.

Crying while I made love to my husband, I prayed to conceive during our honeymoon. I'd even shoot for twins. Dedicated to the idea of starting a family, I was taking a hiatus from traveling. Who wouldn't want to create beautiful babies with this man? Dancing was the world to me, but it was time to put family first.

Later I opened my eyes and awakened with a smile from recent memories of making love all day with an ocean front view. Today's fun activities had me a bit famished. The sun had come and gone, and we had been locked away in our own little paradise. I watched him sleep. Chase and I were intertwined in the soft king-sized bed not wanting to let each other go. His beautiful caramel arms were wrapped around me as I laid on his chest. My frame was small in comparison to his as I lay in the cuff of his under arm. My legs were wrapped around one of his thighs and his favorite place to put his hand was my butt so he could sleep comfortably. This man of mine. I hated to wake him but unfortunately, wifey needed to eat.

I planted soft sweet kisses all over his face, and his eyes began to flicker.

"Well, hello Mrs. Reynolds. Is it time to get up?" he asked.

"Yes babe. We been at it all day and now I'm starving. I been putting in work, now feed me," I said while poking my lip out.

"Girl, you are so spoiled!"

He continuously showed me that I was his world. Thus far married life was the life for me.

Chapter 4
Denise

Years ago my plan was to become an OB/GYN. After I saw how many years of schooling were involved and the rack up of student loans, I quickly came up with an alternative. After researching careers that were on the fast track, my college advisor pointed me in the direction of being a Physician's Assistant or PA for short. Being a PA, you got paid more than nurses who made a nice size salary and you were in school less time than a doctor. Sounded like a win win to me. I wanted to pursue my love for the medical field and make good money to keep up the fabulous lifestyle that I was accustomed to. My parents were glad to let me know that I had a year after graduating to get off their dime. Couldn't be mad at 'em for that. They provided me with a quality education my whole life, and I was not forced to work so that my focus would be on my studies. I did an internship for Dr. Jerry who offered me a position in his practice, which he shared with his brother Dr. Seth. They both loved what I brought to the office dynamic, and it was easy work, great hours, and great pay to build up my 401K and support my shopping habit. What more could a girl ask for? The perks didn't hurt either.

Since my birthday was coming up, I wanted to do something other than host a dinner or have a party. I had been pondering on doing a boudoir photo shoot and I knew just the photographer to help me out. My high school classmate Patrick would make sure I felt comfortable, and he owed me a favor. Being an entrepreneur doesn't initially come with health insurance and per social media my friend was complaining about being sick with the flu and the rates for doctors' visits for out of pocket didn't fit his budget. I pulled a few strings to get Dr. Jerry to see him and he charged little to nothing. To show his appreciation, Patrick offered me a photo shoot of any kind. Looked like it was time to cash in on the offer.

Thankfully my girl Cherri came along to help me out. She always held me down, although at the moment I found that monogamous relationships weren't for me. I had a few boos to fit all of my needs here and there. Truth be told, I would consider Cherri to be my main though. We were more than friends with an understanding, no bullshit! There was no game playing, so the situation was simple. If you had the privilege of fucking with me, it was on my terms or you had the option of not dealing with me at all. No gains no losses. Life was too short for drama and what-if's. The sole objective was to keep it safe and have a good time.

"Denise these shots are breathtaking. I can't wait to put the finishing touches on them. You could have easily become a model," Patrick stated from behind the camera with lust in his eyes.

"Cherri, thank you for your help with directing and keeping the flow going. You two make a great team." Little did he know we were so much more.

As I posed in three different looks, Cherri continuously gazed hungrily. To the naked eye, on lookers wouldn't notice but I knew naked was how she wanted me. Now I just started being plain petty. Moscato was flowing and the music had me feeling some kind of way. The poses got more provocative and sexier than the last. Funny thing was, I noticed a slight bulge in Patrick's pants as he rotated around me, flash snapping a mile a minute. I got both of em going. Humm I must have been doing something right.

Cherri came over to touch up my make-up. I kept posing, signaling for Patrick to keep shooting. Looking into the camera seductively I removed her sundress which invited her to the shoot, making her my costar. This exposed her lavender bra and thong set and extremely toned body. I couldn't lie, she was bad as fuck. One of my favorite things about Cherri was that she was so spontaneous and down for whatever. Standing side by side in lingerie that Victoria couldn't keep secret, we both put on a show for Patrick. I straddled one of his prop chairs with my legs wide open. I wore red sheer and lace in 5 inch heels. My boo sat behind me, leaning into my neck and planting kisses on my left side while her right hand cuffed my kitty.

"Somebody looks wet Patrick. Why don't you come see?" Cherri announced as she invited him over to play.

Putting the camera down, he made his way over to the action. He now had a fully erect instrument we would be working with. Yummmmm. Towering over us he stood over 6 feet tall and his golden skin was on fire with anticipation. Patrick was Hispanic and he carried a natural sexy energy. We took each one of his hands and led him over to the couch to get a bit more acquainted. His pink lips tasted of the aftermath of lemonade, sweet and juicy. Two hands, soft yet strong, of a man who knew what he wanted in this moment roamed over four breasts. He had the body of an athlete with broad shoulders and strong legs, which we kissed and licked thoroughly. That baby arm he was holding between his legs was nothing to sneeze at either. Licking my lips at the extremely edible penis before me, he was about to find a home.

Laying Patrick down on his back, Cherri sat on his face so he could taste her tropical juices. Watching her be pleased by someone else didn't make me jealous by any means, it turned me on. It was time for me to get on the dick. Sliding down slowly and mounting my feet on both sides of his hips to get my positioning, I was now ready to get mine. I bounced with all my might. It had been a minute since I got the D, so this impromptu session was right up my alley. Cherri was enjoying the oral gratification that had her moaning. Funny how Patrick was our little play thing and he didn't even know it. Facing Cherri, we kissed and fondled each other. She loved my breasts, and she always gave them more than enough attention. I played with her clit while that tongue gave her a lashing which led her to explode. She came down his throat and that didn't stop him from going. He was getting it and we were having a good time. Between her sexiness and her sucking on my breast while I rode this massive dick, I was next in line with an orgasm. I came all over the condom that separated us. My juices flowed all over the top of his stomach and thighs. My Aquafina keeps em feenin.

Once I gained my composure from my climax, I got off of Patrick so I could get something to drink.

"Did you think I was done? Get over here!" he said pulling Cherri near him. His forceful tone excited me. Bending Cherri over the armrest of the couch this crazy fool picked me up and laid me on her back so he could have full access to the both of us. He licked the clit and played with my kitty, and it was nothing more than a game to him. Switching his attention, he plowed into Cherri from behind yet looking at me in the eyes the whole time, which showed he wanted more of what I had to offer. The three of us felt as one. We shared fantasies of what threesomes held. Each of us took turns being the main course. No one going unsatisfied.

Fixated on giving pleasure to all invited to this private gathering felt phenomenal. Surprisingly, I felt caught up in the moment. I don't know if it was the fact that dude was laying that pipe to my girl or the way he was looking into my soul. All of the above was unexpected. Inhibitions were gone, and the freedom of sexuality invaded the studio. Two mouths all over your body, multiple hands touching and dancing on your skin. This went on for hours. This was not my first threesome, but the chemistry and attraction had my mind blown.

I was sitting on the bathroom counter regaining my train of thought when Cherri came over to remind me who I was with. She opened my legs aggressively and went directly to work. She licked every crevice of my womanhood. Her mouth was buried deeper and deeper because head was my shit. I could only hold on for dear life. I took it that she saw what was going on between Patrick and I and she wanted to remind me of where home was. Patrick stood back in the cut and watched the two of us. Admired us. Liking what he saw, he slid on another condom and slid right into her with her ass in the air. His strokes were long and hard. She couldn't run from that force with the way he was gripping her shoulders. From her body's reaction, she enjoyed it. She was two fingers deep searching for my g-spot. They both had my attention. They both wanted my all in that moment, and I didn't mind one bit in being the center of their attention.

"Cum with me," he mouthed to me as he started stroking faster and faster making me more excited. I started to feel a familiar tingle start at my toes signifying that climax was near. Cherri was panting because Patrick was beating it up and she was handling me at the same time.

"Ohhhh shit!" was all I could say between clinched teeth while gripping the back of Cherri's neck, making sure she didn't miss a drop of my nectar. Aggressively pounding and shaking, Patrick quickly followed in our orgasmic bliss.

One by one we took showers to wash the day's activities off. I would relish in the memories of this sexcapade, which left all parties well off. Unexpected sex was turning out to be the best kind.

"D, you ready to head out?" Cherri asked.

"Yeah, let me finish squaring things away about the shoot, and I'll meet you at the car."

I picked up his camera and politely took the memory card out. We had fun, but I didn't want to take the chance of having our asses plastered all over the internet.

"Girl, how can I do the edits for the pics if you take them with you?" Patrick looked puzzled.

"I'll send you the ones I want and I'll leave money for the memory card. Thanks for the session," I said, leaving him with one more kiss and I headed to the door.

"All in a day's work, and the pleasure was all mine. Call me if I can do ANYthing else for you."

"Oh, I plan to." I winked at my newest conquest and headed out.

Chapter 5
JaNae

Past relationships don't come close to what James and I shared. Rekindling what we once were had me in such a good space. Okay, getting some on a regular basis might have changed my attitude too. This was seriously unexpected yet greatly appreciated. He knew how to keep a smile on my face, and he fit right into the groove around here. After months of dating, I told Angel that James was mommy's boyfriend. I didn't bring guys that I was involved with around Angel because I would never want her to think having a rotating door of men in and out of your house was cute. I also didn't want her getting attached to someone that I didn't know was going to be around. She loved him and he was so good with her. The only father figure she had had thus far was her Uncle Chase who spoiled her rotten.

James kept me filled in with the situation with his adorable twins, so I had no doubt or baby momma issues. That baby momma of his was something else. I've sat next to him and could overhear her on the phone bitching and moaning about money as if she didn't get $1400 a month. If it wasn't money it was why he wasn't in New York for his kids. I'd seen the deposits from his account, and I had sent his assistant to the post office with clothes for the kids that James chose for them. The kids were coming down for Christmas break and we were so excited. The baby momma wasn't so happy to hear about me, but I just let him deal with that shit. I didn't want to make an already strained situation worse than it had to be by going off on her Spanish Harlem ass, because I could introduce her to the Dirty South real quick. Even after all of that, I couldn't wait to meet his two little cuties and neither could Angel. This was going to be some Christmas.

Houston weather was starting to get chilly outside. Today, sweaters and boots were a must. It was my absolute favorite season. Thick girls shine in the winter baby, and hurting the game with my style was a hobby. My mission this cool winter night was romance. I believed that relationships had to be 50/50, meaning give and take. I wasn't the type of female to just take, take, take so it was time to show my man a little appreciation; he is so good to us. I put together a horse and carriage tour through the Galleria area. It was beautiful this time of year with all of the downtown lighting to keep things romantic. There he was now. That man knew he was fine.

"Hey babe, is there a reason you wanted to meet me at the Galleria outside Dillard's? Kind of late to be shopping Ma."

"Follow me handsome. I want to show you another side to my city," I told him with an little extra sway in my hips as I grabbed his hand and led the way. These liquid leggings I wore had this ass looking good. The black and Gold MK boots put my curves on blast. Because of the night air, my red leather jacket covered my black V-neck sweater over my bouncing breasts just waiting to say hello. We walked about a block from the location where the cars were parked. James looked confused once I stopped at our destination.

"Nae what you got up your sleeve girl?" he said grinning.

"Just a little fun for date night. Since it's cold outside we have a blanket and hot chocolate. It's not as hot as you though." Giggling, I handed him the cups as the driver helped me up. I put my whole ass damn near in James's face. I know, I'm a hot mess.

"Yo, you play too much. You ain't slick Ma," he stated as he laughed at my antics.

"Who me?" I said while I batted my long eyelashes.

"You lucky you cute. I don't let anybody take me on missions, and I don't know where I'm going."

"What can I say? I'm not just anybody, now am I?"

"You right on that. Trying to hypnotize me with yo lil southern charm, let me make sure my wallet is closed. Hell, you already got my heart. Might be trying to get in my damn pocket," he said patting his pockets.

"You know I make my own coin sir. I see you got jokes."

"That's why you love me girl, because I always keep a smile across those pretty lips."

"I mean you cool and all. I'm not blowing your head up!" I said laughing with my boo. He was right though. He brought a much-needed joy to my world. As much as I hated to admit it, I was falling hard. I was scared shitless because of past relationships and bad experiences. Only time would tell, but for right now I was enjoying the moment.

Sipping our hot chocolate, we toured one of Houston's popular areas and our tour guide gave us all types of historic facts on locations along the way. I snuggled next to this fine specimen engulfed in his warmth and Bond#9 cologne. The hand that rested on my knee traveled up my thigh underneath the blanket, past my tights and into my panties, where he was so welcome. He began to press the slippery button he came to love. Torture was not the word as he played slowly then fast in a circular motion. Soft whimpers found no home in my mouth as the cries escaped my lips. None were the wiser due to the loud noises of the city. This feeling was everything. Cold weather, warmth between the lips he was touching, and the principal of adventure that no one around us knew what was going on under the covers. He slid one finger in and out yet, and from the plain eye nothing was going on which made me want to pull my damn hair out because I couldn't react the way I wanted to. He was doing the absolute most! At this point our tour guide sounded like an adult off of a Charlie Brown cartoon. Unrecognizable. The climax was creeping in. My head was now buried in his chest to muffle the ecstasy of me cumming all over his fingers. Wasn't expecting that on our carriage ride.

"Whoo, I needed that sir," I told him while smiling and fixing my clothes just in time because we were pulling up to our first destination for a bite to eat. Handing him a napkin, he cleaned off his hand.

"Hey, I do what I can, now let me help my lady down. Nae, where are we?"

"First stop on the tour is at Johnson's of Houston Creole Restaurant. I'm Creole, so I wanted you to get a taste of how me and my family get down. My Aunt Dana started this restaurant 35 years ago. It's had its ups and downs, especially after my Uncle Sammie passed away who was the heart of our family, but it is definitely a Houston landmark."

"That's what I'm talking about. From the smells of it, I bet the food is amazing. Come on let's roll." Opening the front door for me so I could walk in first, James showed that shivery was not dead. Something else I loved about him.

Aunt Dana was my favorite auntie. She was my Grandmother's sister and a patriarch of our family. She was the auntie that you talked to when you can't talk to your mom. She was there when I had my first broken heart. She gave me the "sex" talk. She gave the best advice plus she would get in your ass and dare you to say something.

Walking into the so familiar place was more like coming home. The walls were covered in family photos showing generations of my bloodline. I really needed to visit more often than just the holidays. My mom stayed on me about family and how important that bond was. Pride covered my face as I taught James the history of my people and recipes as we laughed with relatives enjoying food and drinks. I'd never been interested in bringing anyone to meet my family so this was somewhat major for me. That fact that he fit right in and could hang with them brought me joy.

"Yo Nae, is this you?" James said as he pointed to a picture of me and my mom when I was a little girl. I had to be about 8 or so on this picture.

"Yes, it is. That's one of my favorite pictures of me and my mom. We were at Six Flags in San Antonio that day with Auntie Dana, Uncle Sammie, and my cousins. When we were younger we took a family vacation every year. As we got older life, led me and my cousins in different directions and everyone is doing their own thing. Don't get me wrong, when we get together it's a party but I wish it was more often."

Thinking back to great memories with my mother brought tears to my eyes that I quickly blinked away. I couldn't stand for people to see me cry, so I often suffered in silence.

"Mrs. Dana, this is the best gumbo I have ever had. Thank you for showing me so much love. I will be back for more of the best cooking in Houston. I see where Nae gets it from."

"I know that's right! You betta let em know who's running things out here honey. He's a keeper Nae. Where you been hiding this one?" my Aunt flirted.

"I'm from New Jersey Mrs. Dana, but JaNae and I met in college some time ago. We finally got our act together, and I'm not letting her go."

"Well call me Aunt Dana honey. I like what you talking! Do you have a church home? If not, I wanna invite y'all to come out and go to Higher Direction church with me. One last thing nephew, can you play spades?" she asked him while winking at me.

"I would love to come out to worship with you, and as far as Spades is concerned you betta be my partner or you getting up off the table yo!" he said and they laughed and talked about cards and my crazy adventures growing up.

She was one of my favorite people for a reason. My auntie was a straight shooter with no chaser. She played no games and she would not hold her tongue for anybody. If you could get passed this pit bull, honey you doing something. From the looks of it, James passed with flying colors.

After filing our bellies, we had more sites to see on the tour and the next location was the well-known Water Wall. While we waited our turn to take pictures, a couple was doing a pregnancy photo shoot to celebrate the new addition to their family. How beautiful. I loved making these memories with someone worth making them with. James never saw the Water Wall before, and he liked the atmosphere and beauty. We took a few photos and headed back to the tour.

The last destination for the night was for dessert and a nightcap. James was surprised by everything that I had planned for our date night. I had a lot of fun putting it together.

"You got a brotha on cloud nine Ma. I haven't been with a female that isn't all about what she wants. I should have stepped my game up and tracked you down a long time ago."

"You betta recognize this greatness!" I told him.

"See here you go. Yo ass is crazy. I'll be back, I'm going to the bathroom babe."

"You need some help in there?" I asked seductively.

"Hell yeah!" he said with no hesitation.

Moving from the table to the women's restroom, I checked to see if there was anyone in the stalls. The coast was clear. The point was to be quiet, which was not an easy task. I shoved him into the handicapped stall so we would have a bigger space to have fun. The stall was locked and it was on. As we kissed each other aggressively, my hands found their way to his belt so my friend could be released. I had one thing on my mind and one thing only, to suck the soul out of this man! How was it that James made me want to do things I'd never done before? I just felt free and uninhibited to do whatever, wherever! We only got one life to live, and damn it I was living mine to the fullest. Looking up as I pleasured him, I saw that his head was leaned back and his eyes were closed in enjoyment. I was going to town like my life depended on it. Slurp, spit, and twist move. Somebody was in heaven. I was doing a damn good job, if I say so myself, until I saw a head pop up over the stall.

"Excuse me!!!" I yelled as if I wasn't the one caught red handed.

"Ma'am I suggest you pay your bill and leave right now. I'm HPD," the pudgy cock blocking officer advised us with authority in his voice.

Oh shit, guess that was the end of the tour!

Chapter 6
Chase

To state that I was a busy man did my schedule no justice. Between selling real estate in the great state of Texas and partnering with James on his clothing line, I could barely sit down for five minutes. To tell the truth, I was loving it. I'd have plenty of time to sleep when I was dead. Building multiple sources of income was how to expand and become a mogul. I planned on my money working for me, not the other way around, which was something I wasn't worried about as a young hard head. Back then I thought I had it all. Full ride to multiple colleges, star football player, females at my disposal, and fast money came easy between the pill heads and the smokers. Stupid me, thinking I was untouchable, let the money and the fame get to my head. I was arrogant and flashy as hell. Life was good, but I got cocky. By the end of that epic fail, I threw away my scholarship and any shot I had at going to the league. The worst part about it was that my parents had to put their house up for collateral to keep my ass out of jail. After that, I was scared straight. Had to come home, which was humiliating enough, but I needed to get back on track. My pops had his knee in my back until he felt as though I was becoming the man he raised me to be. As a black man, I already had a target on my back, and it was a miracle that I made it through that craziness unscathed.

Making it through that situation without being incarcerated was my wake-up call. Instead of being a statistic, I chose to give back to the community by founding "Made Men" to create a solution. The program was geared toward young men with the focus on the value of earning a dollar with longevity by doing more than living pay check to pay check. We showed these young men how to build a portfolio so that the attractiveness of fast money in these streets didn't lure them in, how to dress for any occasion, and how to properly tie a tie. My staff and I took pride in showing them how to fill out job and scholarship applications. We lectured on dating goals; do not treat our women like bitches and hoes. One of the most important subjects was, "How to Communicate with the Police". The objective was to make it home and not to be another slain on the 10 o' clock news.

The immature Chase that I once was is now gone and buried. Now, I was a businessman who loved to give back. Did I mention I had a beautiful wife who loved me, flaws and all? What more could a man ask for?

Rolling through the Houston evening traffic heading toward Katy, I thought about my better half. A brother couldn't lie, she was the total package. Bri was my RIB. God absolutely paired me with my equal mentally, spiritually, and physically. With that thought, it was time that we plan some one on one time. I'd be hitting my sister-n-law Daja up as soon as I get to the crib so we could get a trip started. Her travel agency did a great job with the honeymoon trip.

Pulling into the driveway, I got a text from my little Janet Jackson.

Wifey: Come in and have a seat.

Me: No problem babe.

Upon entering the garage door, the aroma of a well-cooked meal knocked me off of my feet. Ohhhhhhh she knew what I liked. I headed straight to the pots and pans. Before the taste test could begin, I got a text alert.

Wifey: I thought I told you to have a seat!

Me: My bad babe.

As I walked into the living room, I was somewhat confused at the scene. All of the furniture was gone. There was one leather seat located in the middle of the room, and it was roped off by a red velvet rope separating it from the rest of the room. A note on the chair read, "Welcome to VIP!" Alongside the note was a huge stack of twenty dollar bills. In front of the VIP section is a silver pole from ceiling to floor.

"Now this is how you start the damn weekend," I said aloud.

Getting comfortable, I waited on the festivities to begin. Light beams started to illuminate the room as Ciara's "Body Party" blared through the surround sound system. Out of nowhere my sex kitten entered the room.

"I'm Champagne Zaddy. Sit back and enjoy," she purred in a little ghetto accent I'd never heard from her lips.

"Damn!" was all I could muster as I watched my wife, oh excuse me, Champagne do her thing. She was wearing a hot pink two-piece outfit similar to a bikini that hit every curve just right. Tracing an outline of her beautifully sculpted body, I was in awe taking it all in. Baby changed it up; instead of her usual short and sassy haircut she had long flowing platinum hair that draped over her right eye giving an Aaliyah vibe. This was a totally different side of my better half, and I damn sure liked it.

As she slowly grinded and twirled around the pole unlike any exotic dancer I'd ever seen, my baby made it look so artistic. The crazy thing was that even during this sexy, sensual strip tease you could feel her love for dance. Two songs later the music sped up. Aww shit here comes the ratchet! The bass dropped and trap music filled the room, making the whole atmosphere change. Champagne unleashed the beast. I didn't know my baby could move like that. The pretty girl shit flew out the window when the beat kicked in. As the King that I am, I was making it rain. That ass was clapping and she had me rock hard. She climbed off of the pole and eyed me seductively. I felt like her prey. As she moved in my direction, each article of clothing was removed and dropped to the floor. I licked my lips while I admired the perfect body before me. Lord did this woman just drop into a split, making that ass bounce, bounce, bounce? I considered myself a G, but damn she had me feenin' like Jodeci.

"Zaddy, I don't see you throwing me a tip anymore," Champagne questioned.

"Baby, I ran out of cash."

"We take credit in the Champagne room," she said, bating those long false eye lashes.

Didn't have to tell me twice. I picked my lil sex goddess up and she wrapped her legs around my waist with clear, platform high heels on. Any other time I took pride in making love to my wife, but tonight it was going down! I was bout to go HAM in that pussy!

Chapter 7
Denise

Enjoying the Houston weather, I let the top down on my 2020 Lexus IS 250. The doctors that I worked with were on vacation, and the office was closed. On top of that, I was off work on a pay day so I had to pamper myself. I decided on a morning at the spa for a mani/pedi, facial, and a massage. This was much needed R and R for this queen. My mood was giddy because everything was in my favor. Just the way I liked it.

I thought I would surprise Cherri with lunch and maybe a little mid-day fun. Why not keep the good vibes going? I had flavor for a few lovers, but with Cherri it was more than just sex. Our friendship was what made our situation work. If commitment was ever to knock on my door, I'd consider it for her. I'd had my fair share of bullshit relationships, so now I put my desire first. I pulled up to the gym in search of a space and spotted her outside. As I got closer I noticed her in the midst of a heated discussion. I didn't know if it was a pissed client or what. Curious as I was, trust and believe I was going to find out. Something told me to lay low and peep the scene from a distance. I parked a row behind them, and I went unnoticed. I was trying my best to be nosy and see what the hell is going on here. The way he looked at her you could tell that he was infuriated. He had the audacity to grab her arm and that was enough for me. I snatched my taser out of the glove compartment and was ready for battle. Who the fuck did he think he was?!

"Cherri are you okay? Who in the hell is this?" I said firing up my taser with a loud cracking noise so he knew I meant business.

"D, it's okay. Just a disagreement. Terrence, you need to leave my job now!" she yelled at him angrily.

"If you'd pick up your damn phone I wouldn't have to track yo ass down. This is far from over. Believe that!" the mystery man who went by Terrance said. He then got into a white Mercedes C class and sped off.

"Cherri, what is going on? And why on earth was that dude grabbing on you?" I didn't know what to think as I hugged Cherri who was now crying.

"I don't wanna talk about it, so please let it go. He isn't worth it." She looked at me with pleading eyes.

"Whoever that was looked like he was about to beat your ass the way he was yelling at you and grabbing on you, and you're telling me to let it go? You need to make me understand what I walked into."

"D, I can't do this shit with you right now. I gotta go." With that being said, Cherri headed back to the gym to leave me standing in the parking lot looking dumbfounded. There went my good day.

A few weeks passed and my mission was to give her space. Weeks turned to months faster than I'd like to admit. Yet there was no word from her. Could I be mad when she didn't belong to me? I couldn't be there for someone who wouldn't let me and I knew when to fall back. To tell the truth she didn't give me a choice. I must admit, curiosity got the best of me, and I really missed her. My fingers knew all too well where her number was located on my favorites list. There was a feeling in the pit of my stomach, which made me reluctant to continue with the call. To my dismay the phone did not ring, and I received a voicemail message stating:

"You've reached Cherri. If you are looking to book an appointment for personal training services, please leave a message and I will return your call."

Unfortunately, I got the message loud and clear. I had to find something or someone else to occupy my time while she was dealing with her drama. Females had just as much bullshit as men do. I was going to let someone else in my rotation to occupy my time for now. Guess you don't know people as well as you think you do.

Chapter 8
JaNae

My mother left me well off after her passing, which was a gift and a curse. Because of her, I built Elevated Events from the ground up and my baby Angel wanted for nothing. Most people would say I had "The Life," yet I would trade it all in a New York minute to see her again. She was the best mother you could ask for. Lord knows how much I missed not only my mother, but my mentor. I was somewhat in my feelings because her birthday is quickly approaching. I learned to turn my tears into positivity after many hours of therapy. In honor of Janice Woods, I partnered with several companies to host a charity Gala in which the majority of the proceeds went to multiple cancer foundations. This impacted the patients, not fattened the wallets of the CEOs. I wasn't just cutting a check and carrying on with my day. My team and I personally visited facilities and the homes of patients as well as cancer survivors. You were nothing in this world if you didn't give back. These were values instilled in me growing up.

Invites to the Gala included my client list, friends, family, and lovers of the cause in general. This really showed me who had my best interest at heart which made me grateful for the relationships I have made over the years, personal and professional.

This year's theme was Rio Carnival. Why not bring the biggest carnival in the world to Houston? Fascinating colors including purple, gold, teal, green, yellow, and orange covered the ballroom in satin, sequins, and jewels. Centerpieces standing four feet tall illuminated with flowers and feathers. The Carnival dancers were what brought the look together. The guests absolutely loved it. I set the bar high and trust, I was a tough act to follow.

Each year we had an auction that featured a tongue-twisting auctioneer. This was always a crowd favorite. The guests got so caught up in the competition of out bidding one another, that they were spending thousands before they knew it. Friends bidding against friends, housewives against housewives. By the end of the night, it was really a big pissing contest to see who had more money. That kept the crowd moving and spending, and there was also a silent auction for those who didn't like the hoopla or notoriety of everyone in the room knowing how much they were spending. So many companies and organizations donated prizes due to the worthy cause. A few local celebrities offered donations or services including LaToya Luckett, Slim Thug, and JJ Wyatt. The outpour of love was remarkable. The list of items for the auction included romantic travel packages, a girl's trip for 4, event planning from Elevated Events cleaning services, a prize-winning dog, gift cards, and shopping sprees to name a few. There was something available for everyone's taste. The point was to dig in your pockets and pocketbooks deep.

The gala had grown from a local event to a showcase of the who's who of philanthropy in the southern region. I spared no expense to show them a good time. Of course, this included an open bar and a meal fit for the elite. My wait staff was dressed in Carnival themed attire as they served hors d'oeuvres, entrées, and desserts.

I was really wishing my better half was there by my side, but I couldn't object to him going to New York on business. One thing I could say about James was that he was always on the move looking for fresh designers, models, and shows. Right now, he and Chase were in prep for Fashion Week and I sensed his excitement and nervousness. We were the essence of a power couple. Move over Barack and Michelle or Ghost and Tasha, JaNae and James were in the building. Thinking about my baby was making me miss him. Those feelings were somewhat foreign to me. Staying incredibly busy kept me from putting much effort into a serious relationship. I'd dated here and there, but it took a strong man to deal with a single mother who puts her child first as well as kept a grueling schedule of a woman who aspired to climb to the top. When it came to men, I didn't want every Tom, Dick, and Harry around my child. I wasn't finding what I was looking for in the men I was involved with. Personally, I had no attraction to momma's boys who thought women were servants to be available at their beck and call, cooking and cleaning to please them. How could my life revolve around a man when I had a thriving business and extraordinary daughter? This is one of the reason's that being with James was ideal. He understood my needs and wants and it didn't make him feel neglected if he wasn't in my face every waking moment. I knew I was not the typical female, at home waiting on her man and ready to pop out several babies. I couldn't help the fact that I wasn't raised that way. I was raised by a strong black woman, and I was raising one as well. I'm sorry but I won't be treating anyone like my husband that I am not married to. Don't get me wrong, I believed in romantic gestures and showing love to someone I cared about, but I couldn't lose myself in the process. I saw myself with someone I could grow with. I would be someone's priority, not their option! As hard as it was for me to share my heart with anyone besides Angel, James had somehow snuck in.

"Well, hello JaNae. It's a pleasure seeing you as usual," Kenneth said kissing me on the cheek graciously.

"The pleasure is all mine, Kenneth. Thank you for clearing your schedule for tonight's event."

Kenneth Livingston was a very wealthy ex-military man turned philanthropist who now resided in Austin, TX. He was also a widower as of a little bit over a year ago who inherited his wife's oil fortune. He married a much older woman whom he loved dearly. Her life was cut short due to a drunk driver. The head on collision killed her instantly. She came from a long line of oil tycoons, so she had what us southerners called "old money". Money that passed from generation to generation. Let's just say for Kenneth to write a check for $10,000, that was a drop in the bucket for him. Can you say coins? I'd known him since middle school, and we were high school sweethearts. Kenneth graduated a year before me and after high school he went into the Navy which meant a lot of traveling and our relationship fizzled out over time. He wanted to marry me and take me with him, but Janice wasn't having it. I couldn't lie, I'd always wondered what if?

"Anything for you, I'm sure you know that. You look stunning, like a million bucks' girl. In all seriousness, I wanted to speak with you. I hope I'm not being too forward, but I would love if you could accompany me to a few events that I have to attend to while I am in town." Holding my hand, he stared deeply into my eyes in hopes of a positive response. His wealth was only one way to describe him. That man dripped sexiness. He was getting better with time. His physical attributes were more than enough to make most women weak in the knees. His smooth cocoa brown skin and chiseled face structure reminded you of Kofi Siriboe from Queen Sugar. He had that grown man sexy, and he was no longer the scrawny guy I used to date in high school.

"As much as I appreciate the offer, I have to respectfully decline. I am seeing someone." I started to blush.

"It looks as though I held my tongue for too long. Whomever he is, he is a lucky man for certain. Now, I'm going to pick my face up off the floor and walk away with the little dignity that I have left," he laughed and mimicked picking something up off of the floor.

"You are a mess. Don't act like that Kenneth," I stated while laughing. His sense of humor was the most attractive thing about him. He knew how to have a good time.

"I do have a few business connections that would benefit your business and charity if you wanted the introduction. That's if it's appropriate. You are welcome to bring your…" Snooping for a name.

"James, my boyfriend's name is James, and I would love the opportunity. I appreciate you thinking of me Kenneth."

"Here's my card. Please let me know if you are available to attend the Texas Oilwell Red Ball, which is next Saturday night, and I have a City of Houston luncheon honoring Mayor Sylvester Turner next week as well. I will have my assistant set up arrangements for travel and have tickets for you and your plus one that will be delivered by messenger on tomorrow."

"Well, you have everything all mapped out, don't you? Thank you again for the gracious donation, and I will await her call Mr. Kenneth Livingston," I told him.

"JaNae, you have the world at your feet. That smile alone will get you anything you want from anyone you ask. You have a bright future ahead of you. Anything you need, I'm here." Kenneth wrapped his arms around me and hugged me tightly as if he didn't want to let go. Our bodies had not been pressed together in such a way for years. I forgot the effect that his touch had on me. My mind raced back to a time when our bodies being near each other was a feeling I had on the regular. Lord, why does his touch make me tingle. This was very unexpected.

"It was really good seeing you," he whispered in my ear.

With that being said, Kenneth kissed me on the cheek yet again and walked away with a wink, as smoothly as he appeared.

Damn, I had to be in love to turn that down.

The event was an overall success. The final tally was $800,550, the most donations we had raised to date. Shedding a few tears of joy, I thanked my staff who'd worked extremely hard to help me pull this off. Without them this would not have been possible. This was a very memorable night, and I was praying that it would lead to more business opportunities. Cheers to great things to come.

Chapter 9
James

Being invited to be part of New York Fashion Week was a serious accomplishment and honor for a designer or clothing line. The Council of Fashion Designers of America held a four-day long event during which designers, models, editors, buyers, and fashion fans coming to Lower Manhattan could see 65-70 shows and presentations. They came from all over the world to review and critique the newest collections. This was the reason I was stressed the hell out. My dream was to create a men's line that men want to wear instead of them being upset when it was time to put on a suit or dress attire. The saying dress for success was a reality. Making connections in the fashion world could be tricky. You come across people from all walks of life, so if you offended the wrong person you were outta there. The most important thing was it's all about who you know. It was far from doing things by a street code, and no time for that homophobic bullshit. You absolutely couldn't screw everything walking. Females came throwing it left and right. Everybody was trying to find a way in. These days you had so many people in pocket like designers, models, tailors, bloggers, photographers, and the list went on. I needed everybody on their job to make this a success. If all went as planned, Fashion Week would put me on the map worldwide.

When you were a black man in fashion, the expectation was urban clothing. My line wasn't for a few men or preppie dudes, it was for all men. If you looked good you felt good. My boy Chase understood where I was coming from even when I wasn't very sure of myself or if anybody would respect the work I was putting in. He fronted me the seed money to get started and out of respect I insisted that he not only take payment but interest as well. For that I would forever be grateful. That was why he was more than the face for the newest campaign, hell he helped me start my empire and he wanted nothing in return.

It was cool that Chase came along with me on this business trip to NY to handle shit firsthand. Helped with peace of mind to have two sets of eyes on everything in the mist of all that chaos. Everything for my business touched my hands. No one would ever say I was bankrupt for giving people I didn't even know power over everything I worked so hard for. Not gon' TLC or Toni Braxton me.

With the show being two months away, we were building momentum for the "new kid on the block" or so they called me. I was spending big money for the latest ads on radio, television, and social media. Failure was not an option.

All afternoon we had been hosting go-sees for models. The thing about me was that I didn't want a bunch of clean-cut Abercrombie looking guys in the show. I needed swag on the runway but a professional attitude. If you came my way looking stiff as hell, yo keep walking! That was not what I was looking for.

Besides Chase and myself, I recruited an old friend of mine who was now a power house in the industry. My boy Larry, who now went by Larenz, was going to help me out with the selection process. We went way back to our college days. He was nobody when we interned and just like that he blew up by styling an up and coming celebrity for a red carpet. He took off from there and Larenz was now the man. I didn't care what he went by, I still called him L. He was a gay black man that wore his pride on his sleeve. That didn't run well on my block growing up, but to each his own. Gay or not, we were cool. L had introduced me to a majority of the connections I had in fashion.

"Yezzzzzzzzzzz honey, show me you know how to hit the runway. Show me what you got!" Larenz instructed the models. It was over one hundred guys there so would take a while. I needed a strong twenty guys to walk for the show including Chase. Things were flowing smoothly and we'd collectively decided on a few fresh faces. The vision was starting to come together.

"Hey bruh, is that your phone?" Chase inquired. Little did I know my phone was ringing off the hook. I was so focused I didn't even hear it. Picking it up off of the table I noticed three missed calls and shook my head. Man can't I work?!

"Hello!" I barked into the line.

"You have a collect call from an inmate in Nassau County Jail. To accept push 1 to.." I hung up on whoever the hell that was because they had to have the wrong number. I didn't know anybody that could be calling me from county jail in New York. Not a minute later, the phone rang again with a call from the same number. Answering the call, I heard the same automated message and something said take the call.

"James don't hang up! It's me!"

Oh hell no!

"What the fuck are you doing calling me from jail? Where are my kids? Yo you can't be serious with this shit!" I yelled.

"Look I don't have much time. The kids are fine, they are with my mom. I need you to pick them up and take them back to Texas with you. My mom can't afford to take care of them long term. I'm going to be in here for a while." I'm looking at the phone in disbelief as I listened to the mother of my children cry as she told me she was behind bars.

"Man, what did you do? Do I need to hire you a lawyer or try to bond you out?" I asked extremely pissed.

"I got caught up with my boyfriend Ren, who is one of the biggest suppliers on the east coast. The house got raided and they arrested everyone in there. Someone who was arrested snitched, and now we're all getting cases. I found out they have been after Ren for years. I'm looking at 5 years. The judge didn't care that it was my first offense. I didn't snitch now I'm fucked. Ren's lawyer got the case dropped from 12 to 5 years. I used every option I had before I called you."

"You need to tell these people what they need to know so you can get outta there, Lisa. I don't give a fuck about your nigga. You been living in a trap house with my kids? Are you crazy? Have you lost you everlasting mind?"

"James I can't say shit or they are gone hurt my babies. It's not a game. I don't have time for no speeches, trust I got enough of that from my momma. Take her number down. Please don't tell them where I am. I know I'm far from perfect, but I love my babies. I was just trying to provide for them," she told me.

"It's gone be okay. You know I got em," I assured her.

"You have less than one minute left," the automated voice stated.

"I'll get at your mom and pick them up today. Call me when you wanna talk to them."

"Thank you. James and don't let them forget me…." With that she was gone. Shaking my head, I couldn't believe it. The timing for her drama couldn't worse. I had no idea what ran through her mind. I sent damn near 1500 a month for the kids and that should have been more than enough help. All I knew was that I had get my shorties and handle my business.

"Man, you alright? I could hear you yelling from outside." Chase asked since I took the phone call in the hallway.

"You not gone believe this shit. Lisa is blowing up my phone because her ass is in jail, and I need to get the kids."

"Man what?! It's always something with that girl. Just go and get my god children and me and Larenz can finish up here. Anything you need, you know we got you."

"Ms. Thang still up to no good? I thought being a mother would have woke her thottin' ass up at some point! Last I heard, she was on the arm of drug kingpin named Ren. He aint nothing nice. He has put out hits on his own family members for owing him money, so get them babies outta harm's way immediately!" Larenz added.

"Preciate yall finishing up while I handle this. Make sure we have 14 from today's group. I want to hand pick a few more fellas from around the way."

"Gotcha, no problem," Chase dapped me up.

"Chile, I understand and I'm enjoying myself. We still need to send over the headshots of the chosen models for the show. Hit me tomorrow so we can discuss the guest list. We need heavy hitters in those seats."

"Alright Larenz, no problem man and thank you again. I appreciate your help. Fellas, I'm out!"

Now I was headed out the door to get my kids out of the mess my baby momma created.

Chapter 10
Brianna

It's time for a girl's night pamper party. I'd been locked away with Chase honeymooning for long enough. My squad was coming through, so we are gonna be gossiping, eating, and being waited on. Since my sister Daja was in town and the guys were in New York; what better time to catch up old school slumber party style? The girls were arriving any moment, and I couldn't wait to see what everyone had been up to. Nae, Denice, and Daja all told me that they were excited to kick it and get some much needed R+R. These days life was pulling all of us in so many directions between family and careers that we could barely get together for birthdays and holidays. We had to get better at making time because life was too short.

The food was done and the margaritas were ready. All diets had to stop at the door because nothing on the menu was on Weight Watchers, and we were eating good tonight. I put together a mixture of everyone's favorites dishes including my famous fried catfish and shrimp, lemon pepper doused southern creole wings, potato salad, mac-n-cheese, and garlic bread. When we were younger, Nae did majority of the cooking, but I must say my culinary skills as of late were nothing to play with. I usually chose more dishes on the healthy side, but when hubby wanted me to throw down, I got it in.

For the pampering portion of the evening, I called up our favorite nail tech. We had been frequenting her shop since we were in high school. The shop had grown so much that she was no longer doing nails; she was a boss with three shops throughout the Houston area. She had no problem helping out when I told her of our plans for the evening. I requested four of her best techs to provide pedicures and facials. I wanted them there an hour early because I wanted them to be able to eat, and I had gifts for them as well. They were working after hours, and I wanted them to know that they were appreciated. Each of the ladies seemed pleased with the Bath and Body Works gift bags. I believe in treating all women special from the janitor to the CEO. You never knew what a small act of kindness could do for someone else.

The doorbell rang, and I headed to let my girls in with anticipation of a fun filled night of laughs. It's never boring when we get together.

"Heeeeeeeeeeey best friend! What's going on boo?" Denise hugged me as she walked in the door looking stunning as usual.

"How you look like you walked off the pages of a magazine every day I don't know. Bitch, you betta work," I told her. Denise had always been extra glammed. I personally didn't want to be bothered everyday with hair and make-up. When it was time to go somewhere and get dressed up I would, but I preferred my natural look. She made it look easy.

"I'm just trying to dust off the BS. Glad I don't look like what I been through. We'll get into that later," she told me.

JaNae pranced in the door with her phone glued to her ear in business mode, spitting out demands for an upcoming event. Lord, this girl had to let up some of the damn time. We exchanged hugs as she headed for the kitchen; I'm sure looking for the drinks. Gotta love little Ms. Mini Mogul. Not following far behind was Daja.

"Girl get in this house! It's cold as hell out here!" I told her to hurry her up.

"I'm coming ,I'm coming. Go head!" she told me.

My baby sister was not a baby anymore. She was a beautiful grown woman. Even though she was a basketball wife, I'm happy she is following her dreams by completing school to become an Occupational Therapist specializing in sport medicine. She also had a travel agency and a few rental properties. She said she didn't want to sit around doing nothing because her husband made good money. I could also call her my Soror because she repped that purple and gold of Psi Kappa Psi proudly. I was very proud she followed in my footsteps, and that made our bond even tighter. She pledged at a Miami chapter because her husband Mark was playing ball there before he got traded to New Orleans. Daja didn't waste her time shopping and being a socialite. She was using her time wisely and not completely giving her life over to a man to provide a life for her. With that hoe of a husband she had, that girl needed a plan b. Groupies and bitches everywhere. He had a 3-year-old son outside of their marriage, yet she stayed. Personally, I couldn't handle the drama and the blogs in my business, but she handled it with class. I would have let that go a long time ago. To each his own, honey.

Now that my girls were here, it was time to get this party started. Everyone took their coats off and started to get comfortable. They knew their way around my kitchen, so as they made plates of their favorite foods, excited about the homemade selection, I handed everyone a bag that included attire for the evening. I bought everyone a one-piece form fitted onesie from Victoria Secret's Pink store to match the one I was wearing in their favorite colors with house shoes to match the sexy PJ's in pink, purple, and black.

"Dang Sis, you went all out for us. Thank you. This is all so sweet," Daja said.

"This is just the beginning, we have more to come. I love y'all, and I wanted us to have a good time so when we get done eating, come into the living room for pedicures," I told them.

"Hey boo, that's what I'm talking about. You know I'm not passing that up. Long as my glass is full its on!" JaNae said.

"Can you put that damn phone down and leave work alone?" Denise said.

"I'm not that bad, am I?" JaNae asked.

"Bitch yes!" we all said in unison.

We all laughed, and Nae put her phone on the charger, which was the only way she could give us her undivided attention. Laughing and catching up with what was going on with my girls made me so happy for my small circle. This type of bond was not easy to find these days. Females were not cut from the same cloth anymore. Nowadays it was about who could use who to get to the top. We always cheered each other on and had been there to catch one another if we were to fall.

Good and relaxed from our spa treatments, we made our way to the den to watch some chick flicks. When we passed the kitchen, I made another pitcher of margaritas to take with us.

"Pour up ladies," I said while refilling everyone's glasses.

"Man, I wanna tell y'all what happened with me and Cherri," Denise said

"How is my girl doing? I need to get back on my training with her," I said

"Girl, training for what? You can't get no finer than you are right now. Negative zero percent body fat," Daja laughed.

"Well shit is not going to good at all. I walked up on her and a dude that I've have never met in a heated argument. She wouldn't tell me who he was or what it was about. She played me ever since that day and won't return my calls. That's been a minute ago," Denise told us, which made her mood pretty down.

"I know y'all are tight, but you have several boo's including that fine doctor you work with so why you tripping over her?" Nae questioned.

"Excuse me, I know you are not trying to say that you caught feelings?" I told Denise. "No way, I haven't seen you in your feelings over anybody since college, hell."

"I consider myself to be pansexual, so it's not about the sex or gender of the person I choose to be with. It's about us being open and honest as well as safe. I'm attracted to so many things about each person that I am with. The difference is that Cherri is the one I want to talk to when something important happens. I didn't expect it, but she is my main. With everyone else, it's just sex but with Cherri we are friends. I'm trying to not let it bother me, but I can't control it. Just gotta fall back and see how it plays out. You don't notice how much you care about a person until they are not there."

"Damn sis, sounds like you got it bad. I know the feeling," Daja compared.

"You mean when you and Mark first got together," I said

"Hell no! I'm about to divorce Mark's trifling ass. I really need to thank him. Because of Mark's selfishness and inability to keep it in his pants, I found the man of my dreams. Gerald and I are in love and we are moving to Houston as soon as my contract is up at my job and the divorce is final."

We all sat there in utter shock. I didn't see that one coming at all. Daja had been a push over for Mark since they were in high school. He was a big basketball star who was drafted into the league right out of high school. We tried to talk her out of going with him, but it was her choice to make. Ultimately, she chose being by Mark's side. As her family, we had to respect it and be there for her if she needed us. They were soon married, and she was thrown into his world.

"Wait a minute, whole up! You mean to tell me that you are finally leaving his ass?" I asked.

"Forget that! Where did Gerald come from? When did y'all fall in love, and yeah I'm glad you are moving back sis," Nae added.

"Ohhhhhhhhhhhhh girl explain. I need another damn drink for this. I'm getting Patron shots. Don't leave out any of the details. I can tell this is about to get juicy," I yelled while fixing drinks at our bar.

"Okay, Okay. Where can I start? It's no surprise that my husband is a lying, cheating asshole. Yall check TMZ so it's public knowledge. In the early stages of the marriage, I was trying to be forgiving because men will be men and this was the world I signed up for. I didn't want to come back home to a bunch of "I told you so's!" After he had that baby on me I didn't give a damn. I got my IUD strapped tight and formed my exit plan. That's why I was so buck wild at the bachelorette party in Atlanta. If he was gonna get down with whomever he wanted, then so was I. It became a business arrangement to me. I wanted to finish school and obtain all of the connections I needed for my business. Being a NBA wife put me in all the places I needed to be for my career. Don't think for a minute I didn't see what was going on. I was just using his ass to my advantage. I have investors ready to take my career to the next level in occupational therapy. I'm starting my own practice once we move."

"Okay Mark is a dog, but when does the new dude come in? He is obviously tearing ya walls down cuz you are grinning from ear to ear," Nae teased.

"Getting to that part. When it came to sex, I always tried to stay adventurous in hopes that my significant other would wise up and see everything that he needed was at home. We'd had threesomes a few times, but it was more on his account than mine. Always about what he wanted or needed. Just selfish. Two women were fine, but when I mentioned us with another man, my needs were obviously a joke. At one point he caught the eye of one of the team owner's daughters. They contin-uously flirted back and forth whenever they would see each other, even when her husband and I were there. They had an open relationship. That explained why he wasn't bothered by their antics at all. This woman wanted Mark so bad that the notion of swinging with them was put on the table. I wasn't with it. Mark just went on and on about how if we did this it could open up another light into our marriage and if we became swingers there would be no need to cheat. Same bull-shit game he uses to get what he wants. After weeks of him pestering the shit out of me, he wore me down. I just said yes to get him off my back. We agreed to meet with the other couple at dinner so we could talk and get acquainted with one another. I didn't expect anything from it. Dreading the dinner, I went to get this mess over with."

* * *

"Daja, you know Jackie and Gerald," Mark said.

"Hello, nice to see you both again," I stated in a non-thrilled tone.

The evening consisted of Jackie giving us all of the pros of the situation. We would not be in the same place at the same time, so that there would be no pres-sure. Jackie and Mark would be at one hotel, and Gerald and I would be at another. During the evening it was as if Mark didn't see me. He complimented Jackie every chance he had but forgot I existed. That really hurt. As much dirt as he did, I never saw it up close and personal so I was very uncomfortable. Gerald must have sensed something was wrong.

"Daja, you look very beautiful in that dress. The color looks radiant against your skin," Gerald said. His comment made me blush.

"I appreciate that."

We made small talk for the rest of the night and ironed out the details of the arrangement. Strictly sex, one night unless we all agreed upon something more.

When it was time for the escapade to take place, you could feel Mark's excitement as we were both getting dressed to head out. Wow, look at the man I once loved excited like a child to go sleep with another woman. He hadn't looked at me that way in years. How did we get here?

When I arrived at the hotel, I had instructions to go directly to the room where Gerald would be waiting. That way I didn't have to deal with the front desk. While riding the elevator to the 8th floor, butterflies emerged in my stomach. Was I really doing all of this to keep a man? After getting off the elevator I searched for room 802. I knocked on the door almost too low for him to hear me so I could go back home.

To my dismay, he opened the door. Humm what was different here? Gerald smiled and looked me up and down from head to toe. He was more handsome than I remembered. He stood about 6'2. Light Caramel skin tone with a bald head and a full goatee and beard. Was I not at dinner? What the hell? How did I miss how sexy this man was? He wore a light red V-neck short sleeved t shirt and black fitted slacks that showed his ankles. The slacks were accessorized well with a black and silver Ferragamo belt and black loafers to match. As for jewelry, he wore a black band on his left ring finger. It stated fashionable but not trying too hard.

I took it that I didn't pay him much attention at dinner. It was hard to see anything else accept my husband gushing over another female. The suit Gerald had on didn't do him any justice, because I didn't get a nice look at the goods.

A baritone voice with a British accent similar to Idris Elba stated, "Hello Daja. I was afraid that you wouldn't show. Please come in."

Closing the door after I entered the room, he surprised me by giving me a hug. My initial reaction was to tense up, but his embrace was warm, welcoming, and very unexpected. This hug lifted me off the floor somewhat because of the way Gerald wrapped his strong arms around my back and forced me to surrender my nervous energy. He bent down to reach my height, which made us chest to chest where my heart damn near jumped out of my body at the mere touch from stranger. I had no escape as his face was nestled in my neck and he inhaled all of me. I could not simply melt at the helm of the husband of my husband's new lover. My body was reacting, which I had no control over. My nipples were hardening against his firm body, and my kitty wanted to purr.

"This is the arrangement that we made so I came," I told him

As I walked further into the room, I saw that it was a suite that included a large living room and a bedroom. It was elegant to say the least. The airy room had high ceilings and tall windows. The space was designed between a modern and roman theme. Colors lied within creams, gold and green. As I looked around, I wondered why I agreed to this madness and asked myself over and over again could I go through with this. This was an awful lot of trouble to go to, and it was not what I expected at all.

"Let's sit down and talk," Gerald asked and held his arm out towards the couch.

"Okay, that sounds fine," I replied.

"I'm sure you are wondering what your husband and my wife are doing and that is natural. We don't have to do anything that you don't want to. I know this was my wife's doing because she wanted to sleep with your husband," he spoke.

"If you know that then why are we here?" I asked.

"Jackie and I got married under the pretense of having an open marriage. In the beginning that's something that pretty much every man wants. Who wouldn't want to sleep with a multitude of beautiful women on a regular basis? As years passed by, I started to slow down in that life. I wanted to become more grounded in our home and start a family. We argued constantly over not being on the same page. Jackie loves attention and there is no level of attention only one man or woman can bring her, to satisfy her need to be adored and placed on a pedestal," he confessed.

"She sounds extremely selfish and spoiled. She needs to come down off of her damn high horse." I couldn't believe that heffa.

"I have grown numb to it. We now come and go as we please and occasionally meet somewhere in the middle from time to time. Don't get me wrong, she is a great friend but the qualities I now look for in a partner in life she is lacking. Being 35, I look for more than a friend. I don't want a wingman, I want a wife."

"I guess I will give you a little back story," I began. "Mark is my first love. When we were younger I thought it would be us against the world. I had this glamorous life designed in my head like Steph and Ayesha Curry, and this charade is the furthest thing from the truth. I smile to keep from crying in a situation that was built on mistrust and lies. Women have come and gone, he has a son that is three that was introduced to our 6-year marriage. This is not the life I had planned for my family, and if anyone really knew the truth I'm sure they would look at me side-eyed for staying." After saying things out loud that I had not even admitted to myself I started to cry. Look at what my life had become. I was trying to sleep with another man just to please Mark, and I had been going go against everything I believe in.

"Please don't cry. He doesn't deserve your tears," he said in his beautiful native tongue. He graciously went to get me a tissue from the desk and handed it to me.

"I bet this is not how you thought you would be spending your night."

"I'm spending my night with a beautiful woman, and I had no expectations at all," he said not breaking his stare.

This was not at all what I thought was going to transpire. I imagined a man going to go full speed ahead with sex from the moment he answered the door. Gerald was nothing like that. We sat on the couch and talked for hours. We didn't talk about our significant others anymore. We laughed and swapped childhood stories of growing up in two different cultures with him being from London and the expectations his parents placed on him to come to America and be successful. I filled him in on life of a daughter of divorced parents who ended up having a better relationship now than they ever did as a couple and having a big sister as a best friend. I let him know that the three of them did everything for me to make life as easy as possible for me so I wanted for nothing, yet I was humble and I appreciated the sacrifices that they made for me. This man had me in stitches and my sides hurt from laughter. A good sense of humor was so attractive on a man. It was approaching 12:30am, and I felt as though it was time for me to head home. I really needed a night like that night, to just unwind.

"I hate to say it, but I think I'm gonna get going. It's getting late."

"They say I hate to see you go, but I love to see walk away."

"You are so silly," I said while playfully smacking him on his muscular arm and blushing harder than I'd like to admit. I grabbed my purse and, being the gentleman that he was, he walked me to the door. I wondered if maybe I could get another one of those hugs.

Standing in the doorway was a bit uncomfortable. We just looked at each other. I was not ready to leave, and he obviously didn't want to see me go. We had started something, something that I couldn't put my finger on. It would have been nice to just continue that.

"Please call me when you make it home no matter what time it is. I want to make sure you arrive safely," he asks.

"I sure will. Thank you for tonight. I appreciate you for just being you and not being a creep."

"Me, creep! Never pretty lady," he said as he pulled me in for another hug. I exhaled all of my worries, and I felt myself let go of so much bullshit as he held me extra tight. I didn't want him to be alone so my arms wrapped around his body. The gesture was reciprocated as well as needed. The tightness of his grip, the smell of his cologne, and his accent as he told me goodbye made me want to rethink my exit. When we started to pull away from our embrace, his lips found mine. I refused to fight it, not that I had much choice in the matter. My body was reacting to a much-needed tune up.

"I'm sorry. I didn't mean to make you feel uncomfortable. I just couldn't let you leave my presence without kissing your lips in fear that I would never see you again."

Whelp, that was it for me! I planted a kiss on this man that was so juicy he knew what was coming next. I slammed that door behind me, and nobody was going anywhere anytime soon. We stayed in a lip locking embrace as we took each other's clothes off while heading to the bedroom. I knew what I wanted, and I wanted him. I didn't want him because my husband was a total asshole. I wanted this man for making me feel like a woman again. Once we were down to our underwear he picked me up. His hands were overflowing with this ass but had no problem carrying me the rest of the way to the king-sized bed. He took pride in undressing me while kissing my body. Now we were both naked, and he just stood and looked at me. I felt somewhat uncomfortable due to his stare.

"Daja, I just want you to know how beautiful you are inside and out. Any man that doesn't recognize that is a damn fool."

A tear rolled down the corner of my eye because I recognized what I'd been missing in a lifeless marriage. I'd come here for one thing, and I got so much more. That man touched, licked, and caressed every inch of me down to my toes. It was as if he had a roadmap to my body and my mind. My skin erupted from passion because I was on fire. There was nothing basic or missionary going on in that room. There were no limits. Being on top I felt free to be in control. Releasing my ponytail, he grabbed my hair and pulled me down deeper and deeper. I bucked as hard as I could, keeping up with our rhythm and getting so caught up in the rapture. My breasts found a new home in his mouth, Gerald sucked on these Hershey's kisses as if he were an infant. My legs wrapped around him, and I saw my reflection while looking into his eyes. My skin felt electric with passion that I've never felt before. He laid me down on my right side and he slid in while holding my left leg up as he gripped my waist. The angle alone had me moaning for dear life. Just when I thought he couldn't get any deeper, he would find a new way to show me that he knew better.

"Shit, shit, ohhhh shit," I managed through clenched teeth. I didn't have to tell him what to do or what I wanted. His goal was to overall please me.

"Let go of all the bullshit. Release it here with me," Gerald said. And I did just that. That was the first of many times that I came throughout the night. I cried again as I released my frustration and Gerald kissed my tears.

We made love slowly for hours on end, which was something I was not used to, leaving both of us out of breath. My needs were put first, and I wanted to give him all I had in that moment and I don't know why. I no longer cared about anything outside of room 802.

Sunlight was trying to creep into our hideaway, waking me from my slumber.

"I'm not going back to him," I whispered only because I knew he was sleeping.

"I don't want you to be anywhere but with me," he said.

At that moment I knew I was in love with that man.

* * *

Looking at my sister with our mouths hung open for once Denice, Nae, and myself were speechless. I didn't expect that tea!

"You can think what you want, but I'm going to be happy. Hell, I deserve it," Daja said.

"No judgment here girl. Group hug," I offered and we all hugged our lil sis and Soror. Damn what a night! We were interrupted by a ringing noise.

"Let me check my phone. I heard it ring a few times. but ain't no way I was missing any part of that damn story. Who is ready for the next round while I'm headed to the kitchen?" Nae asked.

"With that bomb I just dropped, get us all a refill sis," Daja laughed.

"I'll come help with the drinks," I said. Heading to the kitchen we laughed over the news and new couple alert. The drinks were flowing so I was happy that this was a sleepover because there was no way anyone would be driving anywhere. "Let me grab a pitcher of watermelon margarita's out of the fridge."

"You see I can't even have five minutes to myself. Girl I have three missed calls. Let's see who they are from. One from my assistant and two from James. It's odd for James to call me back to back. Let me check on him. "

"Hey baby, I got you on speaker. Me and Bri are fixing drinks. Everything okay? I see that missed your calls," Nae spoke to her boo.

"Heeeeey brother," I interjected.

"What up Breezy?" James said calling me the nickname he made up for me.

"You'll never believe all of the shit going on out here, Ma. I'm trying to get the show together with Chase and my boy Lorenz when I get a collect call from the county. My kids mother got locked up. I got my shorties, and I'm bringing them back to Houston with me," James said speaking 1000 miles a minute.

"Whooo baby. Slow down and tell everything that happened."

"I'm gonna give you two some privacy." I headed back to the party with a new batch of drinks. Nae was going to give us the scoop anyway.

Chapter 11
Denise

Friday night happy hour was calling my name. Much needed time to unwind. My girls were busy with family life, so it looked like I was flying on a solo mission. Glad I kept an extra emergency outfit at the office for times like this. Nobody was catching me out in scrubs, honey. Never know who you might meet.

It had been hectic at the office with it being flu season. This year's epidemic of flu was much worse than any the city of Houston had seen in quite some time. The appointment calendar was full of patients requesting the flu shot or suffering from symptoms. Let's not even get on the insane number of walks-ins that we could not turn away because of the death toll that the virus has taken this year. In the middle of the madness, two of our office staff members fell victim to the virus. My job for the past month has consisted of damn near everything in the office including answering phones, booking appointments, examining and diagnosing patients, along-side administering flu vaccines. Most people think I am shallow or just a pretty face, but I take being a heath professional very seriously. I'd been working my ass off to keep our wait times down while helping as many patients as possible. True enough, I usually pranced around the office being cute doing a maximum of two to three hours of work a day, but you can't blame me at being smart enough to find an office that matches my needs. That's also one of the perks of having your boss for a sidepiece. Dr. Seth was 30 years old and came from an Indian family with three generations of doctors. He was handsome, educated, had long money, and would give me whatever I desired. It was far from a love thing. He satisfied me sexually when I got that itch for the D, and he couldn't get enough of me. I had him wrapped around my little finger. I didn't have issues when I needed time off, and I pretty much did what I wanted. That was just the way I liked it. I loved the way that he was so low key with it so no one suspected a thing.

It all started last Memorial Day weekend. I came in when the office was closed to get caught up on some charts before I went out of town and he strolled in to pick up some documents for a patient. I knew he had his eye on me because he never looked at me too long before he started to blush and look away. That day I went into his office to put a few reports on his desk. As I entered the room he was coming out, and we collided. There was a pause then I said fuck it and started kissing him. Seemed like all he needed was the go ahead. Clothes were coming off, and I was with it. He reached for a condom inside of his desk and took me right there on top of it. It damn sure was some fireworks going on. He wasn't daddy long stroke, but the girth was everything and damn sure was a mouth full. That boss head was really what did it for him. I played no games giving head because I hated when somebody tried to shortchange me. I show out every time or no need in doing the job at all.

I trained him well on how I liked to be fucked, and he buried his face in this ass like a champ. I was gonna have to let him slide trough next week since I was thinking about it.

I loved to catch a good happy hour for the discounted food and drinks. Downtown Houston was beautiful and it was always something going on, from live bands to poetry lounges. I frequented a few restaurants downtown near my job. I'd built a rapport with the staff, and I had no problem name dropping managers to get the service expected. The bartenders made sure I got top shelf, not well drinks, and I tipped very well for good service. Let's just say everybody knew me at my spots. Mingling with other patrons of the establishment was always fun and great networking. I was a firm believer in its all about who you know. Several beverages in, drinking my cares away had drifted me back to feelings that I'd been avoiding. Hard as it was to admit, my feelings were hurt. This was a key reason why I didn't let many people get close to me. I didn't have time for these mind games. The friendship that Cherri and I had put me under the assumption that our situation would be different, and it would not have the same outcome. I obviously read that one all wrong. I was starting to get in my feelings, so it was best that I leave. I was no longer happy at this happy hour so I was gonna order my Uber and get outta there. I caught the park and ride to work and Ubered home when I wanted to enjoy the city atmosphere. My head was feeling a bit light, so I knew it was time to go. Since my car was pulling up any minute, I went freshen up before I left. Getting off the high bar stool I stepped down and lost my balance. Lord I must have been more tipsy than I thought. Two strong arms wrapped around me like a security blanket, which kept me from hitting the floor or injuring myself or at the least embarrassment.

"Oh my goodness, thank you," was what I said to the stranger that was behind me before I turned around to see a familiar face staring back at me. Gathering my composure and blinking rapidly, I began to see red.

"It was no problem at all. Can we talk?"

"Don't touch me. What the hell is wrong with you?" I said snatching my arm away from the man who crushed my heart, causing me to lose my child. "Why in the hell would I talk to you? You can't be serious, after everything you and that psycho did to me. And you actually married that bitch Al," I yelled.

Al was an ex from college. We were young and having fun. Being reckless and caught up in good sex, I got pregnant. My parents convinced me to get an abortion, but after I dreamt about my baby girl, there was no way I was getting rid of her. Before I could tell Al my decision, I caught him with another female who was also pregnant by him. The stress made me lose the baby. After all of that I learned years later that he married her; she was his high school sweetheart.

"Look, I can only apologize for everything that I did. I was young and stupid, but I never meant to hurt you or our child. After marrying Rhonda, I found out so many things about her that I didn't know. If you will just give me a chance I can explain," he begged.

"I don't want your apologies now. Where were you when I needed you? I was going through the worst time in my life. I was carrying your child, and you just left me there alone. How the fuck do you think that made me feel? Not to mention the fact that you had me and another female pregnant at the same time. What kind of shit was that?" I don't know if it was the alcohol or the fact that I didn't deal with the loss of my baby properly, but before I knew it tears streaked my perfectly made up face. I felt like my heart was being ripped out of my chest yet again by memories that were buried way deep down inside that I didn't want to resurface again.

"Ma'am is everything okay?" my favorite bartender Rico asked with concern. All I could do was nod my head yes. I grabbed my purse and coat, left more than enough for my bill, and through blurred vision I tried to navigate my way out of the door. I had to get away from this, from him, and these memories that I thought I buried deep down to not be spoken of again. Thank God my car arrived. Al ran after me, catching up quickly and blocked the door of my Uber so I could not make a great escape. With tears in his eyes, Al reached in to console me and I pushed him. He didn't stop. He insisted on invading my personal space as if he was invited. I slapped him in the face leaving my hand feeling of fire. My fist beat his chest the closer he got to me. I fought him as the pain poured from my heart. He didn't give me much choice in the matter because my efforts to flee the scene were not acknowledged. Once full contact was made, all I could do was weep. Al signaled to the driver that he was no longer needed, and he led me over to a bench on the side of the restaurant away from spectators. Two parents held each and cried together for the loss of a child that would have been 5 years old.

Chapter 12
Al

Moving back to Houston was the fresh start I needed for myself and my son Nasir, who we nicknamed Nas after my favorite rapper. After secrets and lies destroyed my marriage with his mother, Rhonda, there was nothing left for me in the place I once called home in Tyler. Now I was a divorce' and single parent of a 5-year-old. This was not how I imagined my life going by any means. My son was the best thing to ever happen to me; little did I know that he was conceived because his mother purposely trapped me.

Rhonda and I met in high school and been together ever since. That lunatic plotted on me from before I even met her. Our relationship was a set up and crazy destructive. I convinced her to follow me to Houston for college where a whole new world opened up for me. At that point I couldn't shake her ass to save my life. I was coming into my own and the females were definitely feeling a brotha. Of course, I did what any guy in my situation would do. I was sticking and moving with all kinds of chicks. When I pledged a fraternity that made it even worse. Females saw the red and white Greek letters and went crazy. So many girls threw panties at me just because I was frat. I didn't even have to work for it. It was going my way until I met Denise. She was unexpected, and she took me off guard, something that I thought wasn't possible. Being young, I couldn't handle it so I lashed out at her. I drank and partied more and more. Rhonda told me she was pregnant, so I knew my dad would expect me to marry her. That was the kind of men we were in my family. When she told me, she was already three months so there were no thoughts on a way out of the situation, and two weeks later Denise gave me the same news. That was more than enough to take in at one time! Rhonda was not as oblivious to all of my creeping as I thought so she found a way to lock my ass down. She knew she was pregnant at four weeks because this bitch planned it to the T. She waited to tell me until she was three months, so I couldn't talk her out of it. Looking at her you would never know she was hiding a baby. I was really bating 1000. The fuck was I doing with my life?

Rhonda plotted and schemed to get any and everything she wanted. The woman I married was a master manipulator with no conscious. I had no idea until her mother told me from her hospital bed. Ms. Charlotte was Rhonda's mother. Unfortunately, she was diagnosed with dementia three years ago but within the last few months things have taken a turn for the worse and we had to put her in a facility that could handle her condition. It was hard to believe how bad Ms. Charlotte deteriorated in such a short amount of time due to **Rapidly Progressive Dementia.** At one point she was sweet as they came so imagine my alarm when this woman waited until Rhonda left the room to tell me how crazy her daughter was and that I needed to get me and Nas as far away from her as possible. I thought she was just speaking out of her head because of her condition until she told me she had proof. Rhonda's old diaries were locked up in her mother's safe. She gave me the combination to get in and find the evidence needed to prove that the words she was telling me were true. Once Rhonda entered the room, Ms. Charlotte pushed her morphine button for pain and drifted off to sleep as if nothing happened.

"What were you and momma in here talking about babe? I'm happy she has more energy than usual," Rhonda said with a concerned look in her eyes.

"She just asked me to bring Nas to see her, she really misses him," I lied.

"It's so sad to see her slipping away babe," my wife cried. I continued to be there for her, the doting husband. I did keep the warning in the back of my mind.

Unfortunately, that was the last time Ms. Charlotte spoke to anyone. Rhonda's mother suffered a severe stroke in the middle of the night and there was no recovery.

Once my mother-in-law was laid to rest, we had the task of cleaning out her home in preparation to sell it. Ms. Charlotte was in that house for over 30 years during which she accumulated a lifetime worth of beautiful memories. Rhonda had already done an inventory of everything in the house, which included things she wanted to keep and things to be donated. She was an only child, so this task fell on my wife. It was extremely difficult to watch her go through her mother's belongings because her tears turned to screams and outcries to God wanting to know why he took her mother. I couldn't continue to watch my wife suffer, so I took care of the rest by getting a packing and moving company. Things were going pretty smoothly. I planned on getting this knocked out before the NBA playoff game. My boys were coming over and the Warriors were headed to another win.

The movers came across the safe. With the craziness of the funeral, it almost slipped my mind. It was a small safe with an electric push button combination. The code was 227. I remembered that because it was my grandmothers favorite show starring Marla Gibbs and Jackee' Harry in the 80's. Upon opening the safe there were document, envelopes marked important, and several notebooks labeled Diary. The documents included birth certificates, social security cards, life insurance policies, and medical records. The life insurance policies were for Ms. Charlotte, Rhonda, and Nas. All of the medical records were however for Rhonda. Flipping through the ongoing pages I saw that she was diagnosed with Bipolar Disorder as a teenager. She had been checked into the hospital and had been on medication the whole time. How was this possible when the only thing I had ever seen her take was a vitamin?

Not understanding what I stumbled on, I took the books into the kitchen to read. Skimming through them, the pages were dated, and time stamped to record when these events took place. The dates stared 11 years ago. Putting the books in chronological order, I started from the beginning. I turned each page in disbelief of the reality the pages slapped me in the face with. How could I have not known what was going on? How did she hide her mental illness right under my nose? My findings were making me sick to my stomach to the point that I thought I couldn't read any more until I came across a list of names. Everyone on the list was someone I dated or had some dealings with in college, whether it was just sex or side chick status. How the fuck did she have this? I barely remembered all of them. Detailed documentation of how she stalked them all and got rid of them in some way. Pages with their names scribbled all over them with Xs across them. That was some crazy shit for real. Sending naked pictures of one female to her and boss getting her fired. Slashing tires. Running someone off the road. I was sure that when her doctor told her to write down how she felt this is not what the hell he was talking about. She hid her medicine in vitamin bottles. I saw all of the ovulation cycles and play by play of her plan to get pregnant.

Rhonda was not getting away with this shit on my watch. I collected the contents of the safe, let the movers out, and locked up the house. I went to pick up my son from daycare and took him to my parent's house, so he would not be a witness to what was going to happen.

When she brought her conniving ass home, she had something waiting for her. The hatred that was running through my veins made my blood boil. How could I be with her all of these years and not know her at all? Now I saw that the warning her mother attempted to give me was more serious than I could have ever imagined.

She was due home any minute per the text she sent me followed by a smiley face emoji.

"Hey babe, where are you?" Rhonda said upon entering the kitchen door.

"I'm in the den."

"Dang, I haven't seen you all day and that didn't sound like you missed me at all," she said while walking into the den. As she noticed a few familiar faces she stopped immediately. Then her eyes locked on the diaries and pill bottles that were spread across the table. At this point she knew she was busted.

"Al, what's going on? Why are they here?" she referred to her psychiatrist Dr. Cassidy and the police.

"Your mom told me that I needed to get myself and Nas the hell away from you. I didn't believe her until I read these," I said picking up her diary. I began to read an excerpt.

September 23

Today was eventful. I went to my third doctor's appointment and my little one is doing just fine. I've been calling it a boy because I know Al would love the thought of this baby even more if he had a little man to raise. He didn't have much choice in the matter at this point because I'm getting past the point of canceling this pregnancy. Thank God I've been able to watch my diet and not gain much weight so none are the wiser. Accept momma of course. She notices everything. I had to stop my meds, but I've been feeling just fine. I can't take a chance in my baby not being perfect. The only thing standing in my way is that bitch Denise! He is not treating her like the rest of them. He is spending less time with me and more time with her, and I can't have that.

"So did you plan on running her off the road too, if she didn't bow out?" Her swollen eyes were as big as saucers. I knew all of her dirty truths, and thanks to her mom I had the evidence to back it up.

"Rhonda, I think we need to go get your meds adjusted and get you back into therapy," Dr Cassidy stated walking near her at a slow pace.

"I'm not going any fucking where with you. I have a son to take care of. I stopped coming to you. I don't need your help!" she screamed.

"Your mother has been keeping me up to date of what has been happening with you in her sessions, which she wanted recorded as documentation should anything happen. We couldn't force you to come in. Now we have evidence of you harming others, so you are coming with us."

Rhonda kicked this man in the nuts so hard I felt it. As she tried to run and escape, the police had to tase her twice to get her down so the facilitators could get her in the car and take her away.

Chapter 13
JaNae

While he was in New York, James filled me in on everything that was going on with that infamous baby momma of his going to jail and the twins coming back home with him permanently instead of the holiday visit we were planning for. Prior to the new arrivals, negativity invaded my mind, but I covered it with a smile. What if they didn't like me because I wasn't their mother? What if they didn't get along with Angel? Questions swirled around my mind constantly. Either way, I put on my big girl panties and prepared for their arrival. I inquired about their favorite colors, characters they like, and shoe/clothes sizes. Anything to create a vision. I was told to spare no expense and do what I wanted to do. Now, why did he say that? You never let a woman loose with no cap on money when they basically shop for a living. He wanted to turn his guest room into the kids' bedroom, and I did just that with the help of my assistant Amber. We got movers to come clear out the furniture and put it in his garage so we would have a clean pallet. Amber suggested that we use a Paw Patrol theme for the twins because the characters consisted of boys and girls. Great idea.

Rooms 4 Kidz furniture was our next destination because they specialized in children's furniture. They had creative ideas that Amber and I fell in love with. James advised me that the twins were inseparable, so bunkbeds were what we were looking for. We selected two bunkbeds so that the kids would be comfortable at both of our homes. The loft style twin/full bunkbeds were a light wood color called Creekside stone wash. As I filled out the paper work for delivery, Amber went around selecting accessories to go with the bed sets. The kids had rugs, lamps, and book shelves. Seeing her in action today really showed me that she had that take-charge attitude needed to succeed in a consultant position. She had those salesmen running around pulling color swatches and checking to see if items we needed could be shipped in from all over the country. I just picked out the beds and she pretty much took the lead with everything else, and I was watching very closely. She even went so far as to take artwork from the show-room floor. She was making sure that the furniture was age appropriate and checking warranties. Man, she was on fire! I could see that she was hungry for more re-sponsibility. I had to loosen my grip and depend on Amber to step up more at the office if this was the type of work she was capable of. Going from assistant to consultant was not only a level up in pay including commission plus much more responsibility to go along with the title. If she kept things up the way she was going, she would have what she wanted very soon, but not before she got me another damn good assistant. I knew how lucky I was to have her under my wing, which was why I hesitated to let her go.

Next it was time to tear the mall down and get clothes for all the kids. I needed to get Angel winter clothes since I hadn't shopped much since back to school. She wore uniforms, so wardrobe wasn't a big factor for the five year old. Once again, Amber led the charge by checking stores for sales and putting the kids stores apps on my phone. We were organized on what stores we were going into by the floors they were on and how far we were away from the car. This galleria was no match for her. And I thought I was organized. We found 2 for 1 sales, buy 1 get 1 half prices, and all types of other markdowns. We got the most bang for our buck.

What seemed like twenty stores and 100 bags later, we made it back to the truck. All three of the children had plenty of clothes to get them through this fickle Houston weather. It was winter for maybe two months so the twins would have to get used to shorts and sandals with the snap of a finger. Hell, we could have three different types of weather in the same day.

Shopping was fun but tiresome, and we needed something to eat. Maggiano's Little Italy sounded like a super good way to end the day. Amazing food, great portions, and good drinks. I treated Amber to dinner and thanked her for a job well done by getting her a $100 gift card.

"JaNae, thank you. You didn't have to do this."

"I know I didn't, but you deserve it. You worked your ass off today and this would have taken me way longer than one day to complete these tasks. I appreciate your hard work. Speaking of hard work, don't think I've ignored your request for a higher position," I told

Amber. Her eyes lit up like the Christmas tree that centered the ice skating rink in the Galleria.

A few days later when James Jr and Jaden came walking in the door with their handsome father, I prayed for the best. It was now or never. Walking over to James, I welcomed him back with a hug and peck on the lips. Bending down to greet the lively four year olds, I introduced myself as Nae and told them how wonderful it was to meet them. They both came in for a hug on each side of me wrapping their little arms around my neck squeezing tight.

"Hi Ms. Nae," they said in unison.

"Daddy, Ms. Nae is pretty," Jaden said giggling. Angel came over to make sure she was not left out of anything.

"I'm Angel, and I'm going to show you guys around. Come on, let's go." Then they took off.

"Babe, they are such beautiful kids," I said to James as he wrapped his arms around me.

"Thank you. I wish this would have been our lives from the beginning. I would have loved to kiss your stomach while you were carrying my babies and raised them all together. It's crazy the way life leads us, but I know everything happens for a reason. I wanted to be with my kid's full time; I just couldn't deal with their mom. The shit she was pulling was ridiculous. Taking me back and forth to court or when she gets a new dude I can't see my kids, all kinds of bullshit!"

"I absolutely get it. And in another life, I would have loved nothing more than to have not been a single mom from a one-night stand but from that God blessed me with my baby. These kids have both of us from now on with love and a stable environment. We will make mistakes from time to time, but we got this," I told him.

A few weeks later, you would think that they were raised together their whole lives. My anxiety was all for nothing. As soon as I saw those babies I fell in love. They were both very sweet and well-mannered kids. Angel loved the fact that she was no longer an only child and had someone to play with. She called herself trying to take care of them like she was so much older than they are. I swear that child has been here before. I felt blessed at our family dynamic and a tad bit over-whelmed at the same time. Having three little people compared to one was hectic but, as any other black woman, I was getting use to it.

James and I sat down and came up with a plan that was beneficial to everyone. The best and easiest thing to do concerning school was to enroll them into the Pre-K 4 program at Incarnate Prep Academy that Angel at-tended. Usually there was a wait list but lucky for us the principal was my sorority sister, so she was happy to bend a rule or two and she got them right in. Go Psi Kappa Psi! To those who think pledging sororities and fraternities was only about partying in college, please think again. It was about a bond and networking for the rest of your life.

One of the things that I loved about Incarnate Prep was that Pre-K and Kindergarten was full day for stu-dents. None of that half day mess. They also offered after school programs that included tutoring, band, sports, and dance. Personally, I was not the one for the loud noise of instruments, so I ignored band all togeth-er. Having everything we needed made the transition so much better. James and I didn't have to run back and forth to different schools and places for activities. One stop shop. Angel had been in the dance program going on her second year, so she filled Jaden in on the fun routines that she had learned. Naturally Jaden was all in. JJ wanted to give football and baseball a try, so he was set and ready to go. We loved the variety of opportunities the school offered. Some considered it expensive, but I believed you got what you paid for. They offered a higher level of education. Growing up black in today's society, our kids needed a step up to surpass the rest.

Business for Elevated Events went from a steady pace to overload after the Gala. The business was expanding with a plethora of clients with mile long lists of credentials. I would be lying if I said Kenneth had nothing to do with that. I was on the doorstep of the big leagues, and when I reached the door I was kicking it down. People wanted special events to be cherished and talked about by all in attendance and those who weren't invited to be envious. For example, simple baby showers used to be in the home or clubhouse of the mother to be or family member. Now welcoming a little one into the world could get up to the costs of thousands of dollars for a look of excellence. A planner's work was stressful and demanding, but at the same time fast paced and energizing. Staying relevant and on the lips of all was a key element. Having knowledge and the correct attitude to deal with clients made me one of the most sought-after event planners in my area. The goal was to gain celebrity clients and stay paid PERIODT!

Thus far, Kenneth had been a man of his word in helping me with connections. His reach was long, and he was very well connected and respected amongst the black elite. I had taken multiple meetings due to his influence, all with a positive outcome. A positive outcome in my bank account was what I was looking forward to. Now magazines were contacting me to run stories on us as the brand to look out for. I remembered having to pay to get spreads and advertisements.

I couldn't attend the events that Kenneth had lined up in Houston due to the twins getting adjusted. Kenneth invited me to the Austin Jazz Festival to get proper introductions to the Greater Austin Black Chamber of Commerce. They had a reputation for promoting leadership, entrepreneurship, and excellence in the black community. Kenneth expressed they were looking for a flare of something different for future events. Unfortunately, James could not attend because he had prior obligations for fashion week. I explained to him who Kenneth was and why this meeting was so important. He understood why I needed to attend and, being very secure in our relationship, he had no issues because my man knew that I conducted myself as a lady and I handled my business. Bri and Chase kept the kids for us while we made money moves. Thank God for family.

My flight just touched down in Austin, and I was so consumed into reading "Becoming" by Michelle Obama it seemed like I blinked and the 35-minute ride was over. Per my email from Candice, Kenneth's assistant, the weekend itinerary had a car waiting at the airport and my reservations were set for the Sheraton Austin Hotel at the Capitol which was located downtown. Very good choice. I'd stayed there before when I came in town for a Soror's wedding. I understood why it was in the top five hotels. The customer service and how they catered to your every need were A1. After check-in I had three hours of peace all to myself. Approaching room 603, I couldn't wait to take a long hot bath. Sometimes it was the simple things. No clients, no ripping and running, or little people outside the door demanding my attention. Just a little Nae time. I loved my babies, but I hadn't had a moment to myself since I didn't know when. Opening the door, I didn't expect that my room would be so extravagant. Why did Kenneth get me a large suite when all I needed was a normal sized room with a Queen-sized bed? This was way too much. What looked like two, possibly three, dozen pink roses stood in a vase on top of the dresser with a note attached:

JaNae,

Nothing but the best for you,

Kenneth

We would be discussing this extravagance because it was not needed. It was nice, but I didn't really need this. I was just going to head to the bathroom to run a much-needed bath. The first thing to catch my eye was the huge tub in the middle of the bathroom. I have a thing for bathtubs because I love to take long bubble baths, and this one had my full attention. On the counter there were bath beads and bath salts plus multiple body washes of different fragrances. Okay, I was getting a little less pissed about this nice ass room. Time to start my relaxation. While letting the tub fill, my phone rang from an unknown number.

"Hello, this is JaNae."

"Good Afternoon JaNae, this is Candice. I just wanted to make sure your accommodations were ok."

"Yes Candice, they are. This is way more than I needed though. Thank you."

"Your attire for the weekend has been selected and hung in the closet for you. Each outfit has shoes and jewelry to match. If you don't like something or you need something else, please let me know. Kenneth told me to make sure that you were well taken care of," Candice informed me. I hadn't even made it to the closet to unpack the clothes I brought with me.

"Was Kenneth under the impression that I needed clothes for the trip?" I stated with a slight attitude.

"No nothing like that, please don't take offense to any of this. He wanted you to be worry free, so you could focus on your presentations. I promise his heart was in the right place. There are several meetings lined up for which business attire and formal were needed so we got a stylist to look over your pictures and pull things that were not only flattering but elegant," she explained sounding worried.

"I'm sorry, that was very thoughtful. I didn't think of it that way. I appreciate all of the hard work you are doing Candice."

"It's no problem at all. You are one of Kenneth's VIP guests, so I pulled out the red carpet for you. Let me know if you need anything else, and I'll come and get you at 5:30 for your meeting at 6 that is located in the hotel conference room. Kenneth will meet us there."

"Okay, well it sounds like you have everything set up. I will see you at 5:30, and thank you again for everything."

Now that everything had been established, it was time to freshen up. I peeled off my clothes off piece by piece, anticipating the steaming water.

"Ahhhhhhhhh" was all that needed to be said while the water covered my curvaceous body. I ran my baths as hot as I could stand them, so all of the stress and frustration of the world can melt away.

The 30-minute soak did my mind and body wonders. My skin felt so soft from the milk bath that was infused into the water. I also used a CBD scrub that I was fond of. I had time for a quick nap before I secured the bag.

What was it about hotel beds that was so comfortable? I set my alarm for an hour and a half and faded away into another world. Just when I drifted into a good sleep there was a knock on my door. I grabbed my plush hotel robe and tried to gain my train of thought. Lord who was this? I opened the door, low and behold it was Kenneth.

"Aww Nae, I'm sorry to wake you. I was just trying to check on you since my meeting ran long."

"It's okay Kenneth. You didn't have to do all of this by the way. I'm only going to be here for two days."

"Only the best for a queen get used to this type of treatment. Enough of that, gimme a hug girl." Again, he came with all this sexy hugging on me. The issue was that we were not surrounded by a room full of people, it was just us. He wrapped his arms around me and lifted me up on my tiptoes. This was the shit he was known for when we were together. Let me wiggle my ass right up outta this. Pulling away, he kissed my cheek and gazed into my eyes, still not letting me out of his grasp. Why was this chemistry so strong?

Touching his face, I kissed him hungrily. That was all the invitation he needed. Kenneth opened my robe to find me in a barely there gown, which was slipped over my head and removed quickly. This passion had not been between the two of us for so many years, yet it came natural like it never stopped. My head was spinning. Kenneth was no longer a boy; he was all man. Lord, this man had now lifted me high off of the ground. My legs were wrapped around his neck! This was some stuff you read about because I couldn't believe he was going there, but I damn sure was not stopping. Shit, felt too good. I was riding his face because I always say if you gone do something give it your all. He was having a ball with my piercing. I could tell it was a welcome surprise. My moaning mixed with the slurping sounds of his mouth and my wetness was the best remix I'd ever heard. One thing that I saw never changed and that was Ken giving some bomb ass head. I think that's what made my young ass fall in love with him the first time.

"I need to have all of you," he told me, and who the hell was I to stop him? He laid me down on the bed and got undressed while I massaged my clit to keep the momentum going. Once he was naked, he looked at me not caring about my imperfections. He looked at me with pure lust and passion. Returning to his favorite place he nicknamed NuNu when we were young, his tongue was back for more to finish the job he started.

Now I was climbing the walls because the left hand he had on my right nipple was pulling it just right. His tongue was swirling around my clit like a damn tornado and his right fingers were working their way inside me vigorously. I couldn't imagine someone walking by this room hearing the sounds of ecstasy. I was not embarrassed to give into hidden desires. Temptation won this round, but I was the ultimate winner. I felt a tingle as my body started to jerk, and he knew this motion all too well. That just ignited the tongue lashing even more. I had a death drip on the back of his head, so he could soak up every single one of these juices and not spill a drop. The bed was vibrating from my pelvic thrust. No, the bed was vibrating on its own. Was that my damn phone?!

I was awakened from a crazy dream by my phone ringing. It was James.

"Hey babe," I mustered, feeling guilty for the triple x-rated dream I just awoke from.

"I'm sorry to wake you Ma. I was just calling to check on my lady" he said, bringing my reality back to the forefront. I needed that. My subconscious wasn't gonna fuck up what I had waiting on me at home.

"I was laying down for a bit before it was time to head to my first meeting. I needed to get up anyway."

"No problem, babe. Go kill it. I love you."

"Thank you babe, and I love you back!" I told him, and then pushed the end button on my phone. Damn sure had go take a shower after that dream. Whew!

Chapter 14
Denise

Time for a little retail therapy for our upcoming Sorority conference. With the way that I shopped, it would be cheaper to work my issues out with an actual therapist. I'd always wondered why talking to someone was so frowned upon in the black community. Mental illness was nothing to play with and depression was so real. My parents forced me into counseling when I was battling it after losing the baby. As much as I hated them for making me go, I was glad they did. That was part of the reason why I could finally forgive Al and move on from that era in my life. Our conversation was a much needed closure that I could appreciate. Yes, I cussed his ass out at first and unleashed the pain I had been harboring. It also felt good to slap the shit out of him, then seeing a familiar look in his eyes that I saw in myself in the mirror wore me out. Even though I never saw his perception of things, I could now see his grief. It was comforting to know that I was not alone in that.

My Macy's card was being put to good use with the latest sale and coupons. I picked up two sundresses, a

Tuni sling bag, make up, perfume, and a bad ass pair of scrappy sandals that made my calves pop.

My email notifications just informed me that Victoria Secret's Pink was having a sale. Hey, I took that as a sign. I needed some new work out gear anyway. They had tights, sports bras, and tank tops on sale for 60 bucks. I grabbed three sets of those and a fanny pack to match. From Pink I went next door to VS for sexy bras and panty sets. Bras and panties that match was always a must. Not matching your underwear was the equivalent to chipped nail polish to me. Hell naw, too grown for that. I also loved the look on my conquest face when my clothes hit the floor, wondering what I had for them next. Dr. Ken made sure that this bill was paid, and if he had any requests for something he wanted to see me in, he let me know. Perks of having a Doctor Bae.

Feeling as though I accomplished my goal, I was ready to head out. I was a bit famished so a sista had to eat. I'd been changing my eating habits and I could see the difference in my body. Once I put these bags down I could check to see if any of the girls could meet up. Nothing but laughs happened when we linked up.

As I heading through the food court, I heard a familiar voice calling me.

"D." Looking in the direction that my name was called, I saw it was Al. Seriously, I had to stop running into this man.

"Oh, hi. What are you doing up here?"

"Had to bring my little man to get some new shoes, and we stopped at McDonald's to get some lunch. Nasir this is daddy's friend Ms. Denise. Introduce yourself," he told him.

"Hello Ms. Denise, my name is Nasir but you can call me Nas," Al's son told me, holding out his hand prepared to shake mine.

"How are you doing today handsome? It's a pleasure meeting you," I said while shaking his hand. He was the spitting image of his daddy. I hoped this baby used his powers for good and not evil like some people I knew. He was such a little cutie with those big brown eyes and long eyelashes, fresh high top fade, and dressed like his dad in matching red and white Tommy Hilfiger outfits with red Vans. Heartbreaker in the making.

"That traffic is still crazy over there on I-10. It took forever to park," Al complained as if Houston didn't grow by more than a million people in the last five years.

"That's why I valet child. I don't have time for that drama," I laughed.

"You're still a mess I see," he said.

"That's how I roll. Umm, how you gonna feed this baby this garbage? Did you not see *What the Health*? I know you know better than that," I asked.

"Little man wanted some nuggets so that's what I was getting him is all."

"Nas, would you like to go get something else to eat that's even better than McDonalds?" I bent down to ask him.

"Nothing's better than McDonalds!"

"I pinky promise and you can even get chicken strips," Nas looked over at his dad then shrugged his shoulders.

"Ummm, okay I'll try it. Only if you go ride the horses with me," Nas said pointing to the carousel near the mall entrance.

"Wow, you drive a hard bargain, but okay lets go ride the horses." Grabbing my hand, this little boy practically dragged me across the food court to the carousel. After handing all of my bags to Al, Nas and I found the best horses and prepared to race.

Round and round we went holding on to our straps and yelling for our horses to go faster. We were having a good time. When it stopped, you could see the magic in Nasir's eyes.

"Looks like it was a tie Ms. Denise."

"I agree sweetie. Let me run to the ladies room before we go to lunch."

"So you just gone leave me here with all of these girlie bags woman?" laughing, Al questioned.

"You'll be alright manly man," I told him, and then headed off. His little boy was something else, and his smile was everything. What a blessing.

Walking into the restroom I started a little wiggle because I really need to go after standing in the line. Finally, my turn. Heading to the stall I happened to look up and see two women at the sink washing their hands. One made me stop dead in my tracks and the intensity I had to use the restroom resided. Once the woman finished drying her hands, she looked in the mirror to adjust her hair and she caught me staring.

"D!" she said with surprise.

"Cherri, it's been a minute," was all I heard come out. I rehearsed this moment in my head a thousand times. I could hear my heart pounding and my breath somewhat shallow. Absence really does make the heart grow fonder, and I missed the hell out of her.

"I have some things I need to talk to you about." When she started to walk in my direction, I spotted a full belly. A whole baby bump. Cherri was with child. Like far with child. How on earth could that be?

"Obviously, you do. I know it's been a few months since I've seen you, but it ain't been damn near nine!"

"I can explain it all if you can just hear me out," Cherri protested.

"I called and called just for you to have blocked me. That shit ain't even my style, but I thought we were better than that," I told her. This hurt.

"Babe, we are. This was so hard for me, but I needed to figure this out first. It wasn't about you. Plus I didn't know how you would feel," she said placing her hand gently on my cheek.

"You couldn't figure out the words in all of these months?" I said moving from her touch. Finally getting the thing I'd been secretly craving felt more like hot lava now.

"D, we weren't exclusive. You made that clear. One thing that I never told you is that I'm married, and I had been separated for years."

"Tha fuck?! Married!" my voice elevated.

"I know, I know. I married my college boyfriend right after I graduated because he joined the military and married couples get more money and benefits. The marriage didn't last a year. Once he got me away from my family, he became physically abusive. An organization called Carmen's House helped me get out of the situation. Years later he found me on social media, acted as if he was a changed man. We became cool. No big deal. He came to town for our high school reunion, and he asked if he could see me so we could sign the divorce papers. When we met up, we began to reminisce on how things were when they were good between us and one thing led to another and we slept together. More of a final goodbye. Six weeks later, I found out I was pregnant. The last time you saw me I was with him arguing about it. He insisted that I get rid of it, but I wasn't ready to make that decision. The old Terrance resurfaced, and he was trying to force me to do what he said. He was intense as hell, and I didn't want you to be involved because he would have hurt you to get back at me. That's the type of sick bastard he is. After the altercation you saw, he eventually tried to assault me again and my neighbor stopped him. Terrance was trying to push me down a flight of stairs at my apartment building. I got him arrested and had his parental rights revoked. He thought the military was going to save him. They stripped his ranking and shipped his ass to South Carolina so he would leave me alone. He can't come within 100 feet of me or my daughter."

Standing there stunned, I was in shock. I had no choice but to understand her actions and choices. I hugged her while she cried and wiped her tears. Wow, my selfish ass thought it was all about me. That she just didn't care about me at all, but come to find out she was trying to protect me. People were starting to come into the restroom and find our embrace curious. Taking her hand, I led the way out so we could finish our talk.

"Ms. Denise you ready for lunch?" Nas said running up to me then wrapping his arms around my waist.

Shit, I totally forgot about Al and Nasir. I let Al know that there was an emergency and I promised to make it up to Nas. I politely got my bags. He said he understood with a sad look, as if he was looking forward to our outing. Right now that was not a priority; I needed to take care of Cherri.

Chapter 15
Brianna

Time was a tricky thing. It was the enemy of us all and waits for no one. Being home, I'd had plenty of time to catch up on much needed QT with my family and my girls. No more missing important events due to touring. Chase was loving every minute of it and he showed me multiple times a day. I wouldn't be surprised if there wasn't a little Chase in the works sometime, soon and I couldn't wait. At this point in our lives we were ready. I wouldn't mind a house full of beautiful little people running around.

Now that I'd slowed down, I took an opportunity to make a difference in my sorority. I wanted to take more active role than just being a grad chapter member. I currently hold the title of the Southern Region Vice President for Psi Kappa Psi. The southern region consists of all undergraduate and graduate chapters in the states of Alabama, Texas, Louisiana, and Georgia. Psi Kappa Psi, Inc. is hosting our 40th Biennial Boule in Las Vegas, Nevada this year. Boule is a national conference hosted by a sorority every two years. Vegas was voted upon at the last national conference that was hosted in Miami. We had been working diligently all year to make this conference the best to date. Baby, trust was gone be LIT!

Nationals offered more than we could ask for with amenities for bringing the conference to Sin City. We were bringing millions of dollars to the city with our expected 25,000 members who pre-registered. Discounts included concerts, shows, transportation, and penthouse suites for officers at a discounted rate that went for $930.00 a night. The suites slept up to eight. Didn't have to tell me twice, I pulled out the American Express and grabbed my room before they were out. I'd get the money from my girls later. For Vegas we were able to block out hundreds of rooms at a discounted rate with our own discount code of Psi Kapp 40. This was for multiple hotels along the strip. We had some sisters that were bad and boogie and money wasn't a thing and we of course had undergrads that were still in school who couldn't afford the extravagance of the Bellagio and the MGM Grand type of hotels. The team and I made sure we had something for everyone.

Being an officer had its pros and cons. Officers had to be in town for the full five days of the conference, but we did get a stipend of $400 towards expenses on the trip. Hell, that was why we pay so much in yearly dues.

I was apart of the planning committee, which was strategic on my part. That way once everything was approved, booked, and paid for my portion was pretty much over after helping with registration. So I got to enjoy most of the trip, having fun with my girls instead of working the whole time. Work smarter not harder baby!

Daja, Janae, and Denise, were automatically rooming with me. I extended the offer to the current president and vice-president of our undergrad chapter, Krystal and Monica. They were a lot of fun. They took their leadership roles seriously and they were doing a great job with the chapter. I wanted to make sure they got to see the business aspect of the sorority on a national level.

If we stayed in the room the whole week we would have a ball because we acted a damn fool when we were together. No questions asked. There was never a dull moment in Vegas, so my squad and I were in the building. I checked into our room and made sure everything was as planned.

We had the Elite Penthouse. It was a three bedroom, three king suite with a sofa bed, jacuzzi, and strip view. It was beautiful and spacious, so we wouldn't be running over each other. Oh yeah, the girls were gonna love this. Hell, it was an extra $1000 for the butler to be at our beck and call, but I said naaaaaaaaaaaa. I wasn't gone spoil these heffas like that. I was their sister not they momma.

I called my future baby daddy and to let him know I was good. When I called his phone our wedding picture was saved with his phone number. Damn, I loved that man.

"Hello my love," I sang into the phone, smiling and thinking about kissing his handsome face.

"Hey Baby. You make it in okay?" he asked

"Yes love, I did. I just got into the room and it's so nice. It's quiet for now, but the girls get here later this evening to shake things up. I can't wait!"

"Man, y'all are trouble waiting to happen. Just be safe and keep me on speed dial in case your crazy asses need bail money. I love you baby. Have fun," he laughed.

"You know I will babe. I hope you kill the listings you have planned this week. You got this!"

"That's right, the million-dollar listing is the one I'm really after. The commission is roughly around $100,000. So, your hubby is studying this house inside and out to make this happen. I figured it was time to lace my baby up with that new 2020 Lexus RX you been looking at."

"Ahhhhhhhhhhhhh. Really babe? I didn't even ask you for it. How did you know?" I asked all smiles.

"Girl, I pay attention to everything you do. I see the way that your face lights up when the commercials come on, plus I asked your girls."

"You are the best babe," I told him as I heard a knock on the door. "Hold up a second, somebody is knocking at the door. That's weird, the girls aren't due to get here til' later."

"Okay, no problem."

Pulling the door open, I saw a bellhop before me holding a bag.

"Delivery for Mrs. Reynolds," he said as he handed me the bag. I was a little bit surprised because I didn't order anything.

"Thank you so much. Let me get my purse." I was going to get a tip.

"No ma'am, everything has been taken care of. Enjoy your stay."

Opening the bag there is a note taped to a nice sized Louis Vuitton box that said, "I love you Mrs. Reynolds!" Once I opened it, I couldn't believe my eyes.

"Chase Reynolds!"

"Yes, my love? Did you like your surprise?"

"Of course I do. What woman wouldn't like a brown monogramed Luis Vuitton back pack?! You are too much. Thank you, baby. Oh, you just wait til I get home. You must want Champagne to give you another visit."

"Hell yeah. If that's all I had to do to get her, I'll have ten bags lined up on the bed waiting for you!"

"Boy you are so crazy!" we laughed.

"I just wanted to show you a little appreciation and let you know I was thinking about you baby," my loving husband told me.

"You definitely know how to keep me on my toes. I love you."

"I know you do woman. Now go be great. Hit me up before you go to bed."

"Okay babe. 1 will."

I took a quick shower to freshen up and wash that flight off. Then I tied my blond goddess braids up in a cute little bun and put on a purple sundress with gold accessories and gold sandals to match. Purple and gold was going to be the colors for the attire all week because it was the sorority colors. I transferred my wallet, phone, and notebook to my new LV backpack and headed downstairs to our first committee meeting for the conference. Festivities started at 12noon and we had to make sure everyone had their assignments, so everything could run as smoothly as possible.

Guest could attend several of the events, so they were priced al-a cart per event. If they didn't want to miss a beat, they had the option to purchase a Full Access Guest pass, which had the option to enjoy luncheons where we offered guest speakers and workshops as well as parties and events. We had undergrad parties at The Palms, wine tastings with Trap and Paint parties, party buses, shows, and stroll-offs. This week was full of activities plus the flashy lights of Vegas itself.

Only members of Psi Kappa Psi could attend business meetings. These meetings were where we get down to regional and national business. They were long and somewhat boring, but it got exciting when it came down to voting. Some of these entitled heffa's thought they could do what they wanted and jump over starting positions to get a higher seat or rank. Sisters think that they are entitled to national positions because they have been a part of the organization for a certain amount of years. It doesn't work that way. The bylaws clearly state that you have to serve a year's term in a position to be eligible for a nomination in the next highest seat. For example you can't be secretary then be president. You have to follow the chain Secretary Vice President then President. All this drama over titles that you didn't even get a paycheck for. I was good with my position and title. I just sat back and watched. Honey they could have it.

I was going to be working the registration table checking in our vendors until 5pm today then my work was done. Since I knew that this was a lucrative opportunity to make big money, I let my friends and family with businesses know about the conference. My girl Que was going to have a glam suite set up for styling clothes for our plus size sisters, as well as hair and makeup for her brand Beatz on Q. She started out by catering to plus-sized women. A lane that she excelled in. This was one thick woman that looked on point for every occasion. Random people stopped her constantly and asked where she purchased an outfit or who did her makeup, and this was where she started with majority of her clients. Looking at her sells her brand every time, so she didn't leave the house with a hair out of place. Lord, I didn't see how she did it. I was known to throw on a cap and run to the store. Our chapter president Krystal from undergrad was a part of her glam squad because she was a phenomenal makeup artist. Why not put two like-minded people together?

My God sister Shan owned a bakery in Atlanta called Delightful Confections that specialized in cakes, desserts, and treats to make every event one to remember. Her cakes were not only beautiful, but they tasted amazing. We were able to work out a hefty contract for her company to handle all the desserts for the conference. That girl didn't play about her business or her money, so I couldn't wait to see what she came up with. I knew I was going to gain ten pounds messing with those cookies and DC krispie treats; they are my favorites. Her company made my wedding cake, grooms' cake, and candy table for my wedding. I didn't know what was talked about more from the wedding, my barely there dress or her cakes.

Another good friend of mine was an artist of all sorts, she designed jewelry and accessories, handbags, and she created paintings on-site. Taylors brand is Touched by Tay and all of her pieces were eclectic, handmade, and one of a kind. I told her to buy up every piece of purple and gold everything material she could find. My sisters lived for Psi Kappa Psi items that no-body else had. For my wedding gift, Taylor gave us a painting of us from our first date. It brought me to tears instantly. Baby girl was crazy talented.

Finally, I couldn't leave my favorite cousin at home. Wayne was the king of Shirt Trappin, as he called it. I remembered when Wayne got his first heat press and started his local t-shirt business for a few rappers and local businesses in the city, and three years later he had a warehouse and people on payroll completing massive orders for screen print and embroidery. It was family run and operated. Each registered Psi Kappa Psi mem-ber got one of three custom shirts from Lewis Custom Designs in her swag bag. He would also have a booth set up to sell shirts, bags, backpacks, hats, embroidered jackets, and other Psi Kappa Psi apparel. Pretty much anything these ladies could ask for would be at their fingertips. I knew my team was ready. We had a total of twenty-five vendors to provide any and everything a woman would need.

Looking at my AppleWatch, I saw the time was now 5:30. My work was done for registration, so as far as I was concerned, it was time to kick it. All but three ven-dors registered on time. We had a few late registrations due to flight delays.

We had a meet and greet tonight, and my girls should arrive to the room shortly. They had key cards at the front desk so that they wouldn't have any issues settling in. Lord only knew what we are about to get into. I was stopping at the liquor store to get bottles. We needed some Crown Apple and Crown Peach, plus Watermelon, pineapple, and Amoretto Cîroc on deck for sure. JaNae was the mixologist in the group, so the cumfoolery was about to get real. I'd already called room service and had them bring us soda and juices for our drinks.

Swiping my key card in the elevator, I headed up to our quarters. After a few upward movements the doors open at our rooms. I was greeted with the banging sounds of Nipsey Hussle's "Last Time that I Checked". One of our favorite songs to step too. Damn that brother was loved, a soul that was lost way too soon. He was a real dude who went from gang banger to helping his community. Gotta respect that.

As I walked into the kitchen, I saw that all of the girls were there and accounted for. They were in there getting it, doing Psi Kappa Psi strolls around the island in the middle of the room.

"I see that party started without me," I said to my sorors with a playful attitude.

"Heeeeeeeeeeeeeeeeeey Sis!" Everyone said in unison, which was one of our national greetings towards another sister of Psi Kappa Psi. Everyone came in for hugs. I truly loved these ladies and what our sisterhood and bond represented.

"Pour up sis!" Denise said.

"I got the gummies on deck for the trip for y'all. My cousin Stacy picked me up from the airport this morning, so I went to visit the family and she put me on with her plug," Krystal gladly informed us showing us the colorful weed laced treats. Last time I had some of those, I had some of the best sex of my life, then cleaned my house from top to bottom with the excess energy. Chase was knocked out from the work out I gave him. I damn sure was gonna eat some this weekend, and probably take a few home.

"Shit, I'm down for a good time but I'm telling you now, you bet not get out of hand and look out for each other!" JaNae never misses a moment to be the mother in the crew. Lol gotta love her.

"Yes, Big Sister "Poetic Justice!" I told her laughing.

"My friend Lana lives here now, and she is a part of the Cirque De Solei Zumanity show at New York New York Hotel. Would y'all like to go check it out with me after the meet and greet tonight?" I asked.

"Of course! Sis I wanna learn some new moves from that sexy show to put on Bae. Owwwwwwwwww," Daja said in a Cardi B fashion. She was absolutely loving her new life with her new man, and I couldn't blame her.

"I better get it in tonight because I'm here to work the rest of the weekend. I plan on beating these faces to the gawds. Trust me, I'll be having all of you ladies on point. You guys better book your appointments early," Krystal let us know. "I wore Sephora out, and I ordered all of my favorite make up brands to create looks from glamorous to natural looks. Crayon Case by Wuzzam Supa is my secret weapon to make these purple and gold eyelids really pop."

"We are going to support you sis. You know you can count on us," Monica assured her.

"We definitely got you sis. I wanted to make sure you were in an amazing position for money to be made and you are. You will leave here with thousands on deck. Just trust your big sis," I told Krystal.

"That's what I'm talking about!" Krystal high fived me.

"Let's get the party started. Heeeeeeeeeeey Sis!" Denise said.

"Heeeeeeeeeeeeeeeeeeeeeeeeeeeey Sis!" we all shouted.

Chapter 16
Krystal

I'd never been to Vegas before, so I was ready to see what it was all about. I appreciated the fact that Bri invited Monica and myself to learn more about the sorority that we loved so much. I couldn't afford the trip on my own, so staying with the girls in this glammed-up penthouse was doable on our pockets. I was always down for new ideas on how to make our chapter bigger and better. This year's focus was quality over quantity. I had no desire to be the biggest sorority in our area if people didn't put in the work. These females thought that wearing Greek letters, stepping, and looking pretty was all it was to it, when it wasn't. We took an oath of leadership and citizenship, promising to serve our community. As president of The University of Houston Psi Kappa Psi undergraduate chapter, I took those things to heart. Business first and party later. If you could be all over Snapchat partying, I expected that same energy at a community service function. If not you were cool, you would get a fine and you would not be allowed to attend our next party in any gear or step.

We didn't half ass anything. Since I had been president we had been nationally recognized for our service efforts in multiple publications. I was looking forward to gaining knowledge to push my sorors further under my leadership.

Having a much-needed break from H-town was cool; I just hoped that there were no issues with Monica. She could be a little, shall I say, boy crazy. She was always on the prowl, like a dude or something. It was all about her being the center of attention or she had a whole attitude. I damn sure didn't have the time for that because I came out here to hustle and make a name for myself. Monica was my girl, but one day that shit was going to put her in a situation she couldn't get out of.

Being a makeup artist, I didn't want my artistry to just be local. I tried the makeup counter action at the mall, but it wasn't for me when I can make more money an hour on my own. You want me to stand all day doing makeovers while making $12.00 an hour? Naw, that wasn't adding up to me when working on my own I started out at $30.00 per person, now ranging $75.00 to $100.00 depending on mobile service. That sounded more like it if you asked me. My plan was to build a name for myself in the industry. I was trying to get flewed out, as they say. Catch me at the Grammy's, Stellar's, and on movie sets. I was trying to gain celebrity clients and stay paid. Make-up artists were usually in the background and that's how I liked it. Long as my checks cleared, I never had to see the limelight. My work spoke for itself. I was already IG verified with my makeup videos and tutorials. I didn't have to post not one half naked pic or twerk video to achieve it.

Participating in this glam suite was going to create more opportunity for me and my brand. We have Sorors who have plugs everywhere, and I was ready to be put on. Next year I'd be done with school, so I was trying to get all of my ducks in a row to have myself set after walking across that stage. I was graduating with a business degree in addition to my obtaining Esthetician license. I stayed on top of my craft by finding new techniques for skin care as well as make-up. It hadn't always been easy with the creation of the YouTube MUA's, but professionalism separated the real from the fakes. Anyone could draw on uneven brows and cake on makeup, but could they blend colors to match all skin tones and give direction for natural skin care? All make up brands did not fit all skin types and that was what a customer got with me. A true artist could work with more than one ethnicity and hold a variety of looks for all of them. Thus far I held skin care, make up, and lash extensions under my belt for my list of services and it was going to keep growing. I was headed towards my micro-blading certification as well. I planned on being a one stop shop for beauty.

Sisterhood and work were not the only reasons I'd come on this trip. Bae was in town for business, so I gotto spend some QT with him as well. Our relationship was not one that I broadcasted to the world because I didn't particularly care for people being in my relationship. Being as though he was six years older than me, he carried himself differently than those pions I went to school with. He treated me well, he believed in me, and we shared the same visions on creating a family. His sexy was so serious with his bald head and sprinkle of gray in his beard. He was a part of the well-known beard gang group, and those green-hazel eyes mesmerized every female in his path. Mature but fine. That man worked out religiously, and he had no problems lifting my thick frame. I was tall, so I carried it well. Small waist and I was thick in all the right places. He smacked this voluptuous ass with everything he had when the mood was right. He loved this thickness and, he can't get enough of these 42 triple D's.

The thing about it was, it wasn't just the sex. Sex was only a king-sized plus. He stimulated my mind and took me places dudes my age couldn't even fathom. Every time he was with me he checked to see how much gas was in my car and if it was below half a tank he filled it up. Bae studied with me to help me prepare for tests. He bathed me to help me relax my mind before a sensual massage. If we came back around to the subject of sex, sprung was what you called it. How that man knew his way around the female form like he did, I didn't know. It was anything goes. Open minds only, get ready for the adventure or don't enter the room. I was told this early on. No such word as no. Bae made sure to keep me comfortable and wouldn't put me in a position to have to doubt. All I could do was enjoy the ride. Ohhhhhhhh and what a ride it was. He made love to my mind and he straight blew my back out. Baby got STAMINA FOR DAYS! I could never look at guys my age the same. It was cute how the tried to step to me and actually think they had a chance. I just chuckled and kept it moving. Baby, I fucked with a grown ass man.

Drinks were flowing, the gummies were kicking in, and we were having a great time. It was nice to be at a sorority function and be on the sidelines. You got the opportunity to network with people from all over the country and enjoy what was going on. Usually I was stressed over everything running the way it should be. This might be a social, but I was out here on my grind. I was now booked for the duration of the time while would be here because I was passing out cards and setting appointments left and right. My look tonight was everything. Had to pull out an extravagant face to show the ladies what I was working with. They weren't ready for the glammed out purple glitter beat and Lash+Fetish 3D Mink lashes. Only lashes I worked with. For the first five people that booked I threw in lashes for free. Word got around fast. I was killing it, so my sorors had to stop and ask. I gladly informed them about the glam suite and how to book me because spots were filling up fast. Mission accomplished!

Making my way to the bar, I saw the girls and I needed to sit for a minute. My heels were wearing me out. Bet I was switching to my Vans when we hit the strip. Damn.

"I'm feeling so good right now," Ja'Nae said.

"I can't even believe you had any gummies," Denise told her

"When in Rome, fuck it! I get tired of being the sensible one all the damn time," Ja'Nae laughed.

"It's some cuties up in here, that's all I know. If I don't come back to the room, I'll keep y'all posted. I'm about to go make my rounds, let em see who is in the building ok!" Monique informed us. Lord that girl hot ass stayed on one.

"That thang right there is a whole mess," Bri laughed. Little did Bri know how right she was.

Bobbing my head to the music, the DJ had it jumping in there. Kicking it with my girls on some drama free stuff, that was how you partied. Everyone got up to stroll with the rest of our sorors as the party elevated. I stayed to keep our table plus my feet were still a bit tired from all of that networking. The cuter the heels the more painful. Life of a bad ass!

While sipping my drink and vibing out, my peripherals observed a sexy piece approaching. Licking my shimmery glossed lips, I prepared for this interaction.

"Is this seat taken?"

"No, not at all," I stated looking him up and down hungrily. I knew where I'd like to sit. Right on his damn face.

"I don't mean to bother you, but I saw you sitting here from across the bar and you took my breath away. You are stunning," Well damn! That's how you get approached in Vegas? Looks like my kind of town.

"Thank you. You are going to make me blush," I said

"I had to come over and say something. A few of these ladies were pretty upset that I wouldn't entertain what they were trying to throw at me because my focus was on you."

"I'd like them to gladly get outta my man's face." I stood up to embrace my boo, laying a deep kiss on him so if anyone was watching, these heffas would know that this one was off limits. I was usually not one for PDA, but I had to make a point.

"Can we take this conversation back to my suite?"

"Okay baby, let me just tell my girls that I'm not going to the show with them after the party." I sent a quick text to let the group know I found something delicious to get into.

"You were really working the room, handling your business babe. Your makeup is beautiful, so I know they will be beating down your door. That's how you get out here and grind. I'm proud of you," my love told me.

"You can show me better than you can tell me," I said real slick letting him know I was more than ready to exit. I finished my drink so we could go do what grown folks do. I had an early day tomorrow, so I couldn't be up all night playing with Bae. Bri was coming in our direction. She must have gotten my text about not coming to the show.

"Hey cousin, you having a good time? Do you have everything you need for tomorrow?" Bri asked.

I damn near choked on my drink.

"Cousin?" I mustered out.

"Umm, yeah. Wayne is my cousin. Wait a minute, is this who you were ditching us for to go creep with?" Bri asked. She didn't look too happy about this little discovery.

"I had no idea that y'all are related sis."

"The both of you are grown so this is not my business. Wayne let me holla at you for a minute," Bri asked and they both walked outside. *Why would she be that upset?* I wondered to myself as they walked away.

"How can I help you BriBri?" Wayne asked in an annoying tone.

"Look here cousin, I don't need you wrecking this girl's world with yo married ass. That's my Soror and I'm gone be the one here stuck picking up the pieces once you break her heart. Man, I called you out here to promote your business not to fuck all of my sisters!"

"I didn't know anything about y'all being in the same sorority. You act like I go to school with you or something. Plus, I'm separated. Me and Tia are through. I learned the hard way you can't turn a hoe into a housewife," Wayne protested.

"You have said that shit before. I don't know what magical unicorn pussy powers Tia has over you, but it's like you can't leave her trifling ass alone. I don't want Krystal to be another one of your casualties."

"You don't have to worry about Krystal. The only thing Tia and I have to talk about is the kids. I'm not dipping over there or anything, and it's fucking her head all the way up. I strictly do for my kids then I'm out. No overnight stays no none of that. She needs to get it through her thick skull that I'm done. Just don't have time for that shit anymore."

"That's what ya mouth say. I'll believe it when I see it," Bri said rolling her eyes.

"Magical Unicorn Pussy huh?!" Wayne cracked up and Bri joined him.

"Boy yo ass is crazy. Let's go."

The cousins shared a laugh before heading back to the party. One thing about them, they could disagree, and it was all love because they were so tight.

Chapter 17
Monica

No, the fuck this bitch didn't. Krystal saw me talking to that cutie with the green eyes at the bar and now she was all up in his face. I thought that was my girl and now she was blocking. Man, I didn't take that disrespect from no damn body. Thought this Vegas trip was gonna be fire, but this was only day one and I was already pissed off. I was gonna make sure her ass knew it too.

I was the type of female that didn't have to wait for a guy to make the first move. I went after what I wanted. Sometimes it was the chase of it. The chase turned me on. Some called that forward, but I just looked at it as doing me. What was the point of playing games when the whole point of dating was eventually to fuck anyway? I kept it safe because you could be a sexual beast and be disease free without taking multiple trips to the clinic. I didn't have time to be ya baby momma. Hell, I wasn't even trying to be your boo. It was easier to stick and move. You're only young once and I was gonna have all the fun I could now.

The sexiness of the Zumanity show had me a little hot and bothered. It was a bunch of dancers dressed in sexy clothes damn near having an orgy. Who wouldn't be turned on by that? Looking around the room I could tell I wasn't the only one. A very attractive white guy locked eyes with me a few times during the show. I excused myself from my sisters and exited to the bathroom, giving him a head nod to follow me. Let's see if he was bout that life. Was I supposed to give two shits about who he was with? If so, I didn't! Walking into the hallway, I saw him trail me with enough distance to see where I was going but not make it apparent that we were going to the same location. The family bathroom had enough space to do what I had in mind. The blond, tall glass of water who was following me entered the family space.

"Hey, I'm Justin. What's your name beautiful?" he asked as if I was awaiting his introduction. The way he carried himself showed that he had swag. He was white, but he had a little soul in him. Wasn't trying to be black, but he definitely had a bit of black influence. Channing Tatum came to mind.

"Lock the door behind you. I have one question Justin: do you eat pussy?"

"Most definitely," he said looking me up and down like he was ready to digest his last meal. The clicking sound of the lock made me aware that the door was secured. Didn't need anyone to be busting in because I wasn't in the mood to be watched tonight. Maybe some other time. I pushed the extravagant baby changing materials off of the counter so I could let all of my frustrations rain down. Justin pulled my panties off and threw my right leg over his shoulder. A smile crept across his face as he notices the smooth bearings of my waxed chocolate lips.

"You are dripping already, and I haven't touched you yet. That's what I like to see," he said.

"That's my secret sauce. Try it."

He took one extremely long lick, which wet me from my ass to my clit. I knew I was messing with a pro. He buried his face in my shit so tough you would think a grand prize was waiting on him when he got done. Gripping my ass, he sent a shiver up my spine. I held one hand on the counter top and the other around his neck to keep that mouth secure. How the fuck was he swirling his tongue and sucking my shit at the same time? The intensity on this heat had me wanting more and more. I started riding his face, which made him go even harder. I didn't know Justin was gone come in here on his A game like this. Licking, swirling, and sucking in a gravitational pull with my clit. My God this couldn't be real. I done had some pussy monsters in my day, but none like this.

"Shit, I know you like it," he bragged.

I couldn't even talk shit because the fool's head game was so good. Justin removed my legs that were wrapped tightly around his neck and bent me over the counter. He opened up the cheeks and ate it from the back.

He took me by surprise on that one. I was starting to tingle all over. He was taking way too much control for me, and I hated to relinquish that much of myself to anyone no matter how good the sex was. As I tried to scoot out of his embrace before I fell prey to his tongue lashing, he got back on that clit. I took my left breast out and begin to squeeze my nipple, which intensified my orgasm. The rainforest was about to begin, and I hoped he was ready. Lord, he felt that first shiver of my body and clamped down, preparing to take it all in. Holding the back of his head tightly to match the intensity of my volcanic eruption, my screams bypassed the locked door. Feelings of euphoria was what climaxing felt like. The best damn feeling in the whole wide world. How had no one bottled that shit? It would sell more than Viagra.

"Whoo Justin, you are something else honey!"

"I aim to please, and it's way more where that came from," he said gripping a nice size looking package through his shorts. His face was glistening from my juices, which he seemed to enjoy. Mr. Justin ain't nothing nice okay.

"As tempting as that sounds, I have to take a raincheck love," I told him while getting myself together in the mirror. Justin came behind me with a very sexy smile and began to rub that monster he was gripping on my ass, looking at me in the mirror the whole time. It was already so warm in this bathroom, and he was not helping things at all.

"Just in case you change your mind, here is my number. I feel like this is more of a to be continued situation." He was cleaning himself up, but giving me a sexy glare the entire time.

"Do you now? All I can say is we shall see." We exchanged phone numbers, and I prepared to make my exit. The boy was good, so I might just have to take him up on that offer. Gave him a kiss then I was out.

I returned to my seat as if nothing ever happened. Looked like the show had just finished. I was right on time for a standing ovation.

"Soror you cool?" Daja asked me.

"Girl yes, had to run to the restroom then take a phone call. What did I miss?"

"Zumanity lives up to all of the hype. I see why thousands of people see this show every week. I need another drink after that and a cold shower," Daja said, making the crew laugh. Boy did I agree with her as I smirked to myself.

Chapter 18
JaNae

After being in meetings for two days straight, watching the insanity of elections I was happy that I choose to stay out of the political aspect of Greek life. Members politicked and fought for seats to make decisions for thousands of people. Note, there was no paycheck attached. Officers only had dues waved and got stipends for trips. That sounded like more of a headache to me than anything. Hell, it was hard enough deciding what to make for dinner for the four other people in my house. Bri kept her title of Vice President of the Southern Region, which she seemed just fine with.

I spent more than enough money on Psi Kappa Psi paraphernalia no thanks to Wayne and that included the family discount. That $450.00 tab included T-shirts and keychains that I purchased for all of the girls to signify our trip. I hadn't bought any paraphernalia in so long. I didn't have anything up to date to wear when I did get to attend Psi Kappa Psi events. It was all well worth it.

Now had come the time to unwind, and I was sipping drinks by the pool with my girls. To be honest, I couldn't even remember the last trip we took together, which said a lot. Bri didn't give us a choice or option in the matter for this year's boule'. She advised us to drop everything that we were doing and to make it happen, which all of us did. When she put her foot down, she would not take no for an answer so she would have bugged the hell out of us until we made it work.

With everything life had been throwing our way, we haven't made the importance of our bond a priority. We had to do better.

"Ladies, we don't get together as often as we used to. This trip reminded me of how much I miss seeing you heffas all the time. I vote that right here right now we vow not to let life get in the way of the sisterhood. Let's have Daja put that travel agency of hers to good use and start booking at least one solid trip a year somewhere in this big beautiful world. Time to get some stamps on our passports. We can alternate family trips and girls trips so everyone we love is included. Y'all down?" I asked.

"Toast to the sisterhood, count me in. You know I'm always down for a reason to tear the mall down," Denise added while raising her glass.

"We are definitely down," Krystal added on behalf of her and Monica.

Thought I caught a slight side eye from Monica, but I might have been tripping, LITERALLY. I done had some CBD oil under my tongue that I got from Fremont Street. I was feeling pretty good.

"You know I got you covered, sis. My mind is already thinking about packages for New Orleans, Miami,

Jamaica, and St. Lucia. I can check it out and get back to everyone with the deets once we get home because a bitch is on vacation dawg!" Daja's crazy ass informed us.

All of the ladies agreed. I really didn't know what I would do without them. Before there were James, and the twins and Angel were even thought of, I had my crew.

"Since it's our last night in town I charted a party bus and its scheduled to arrive at 10pm. We have three hours to get ready for the Psi Kappa Psi Farewell party. Get sexy cuz it's about to go down. I call first in your chair Krystal. Do whatever look you want honey because we know I'm gone be cute regardless," Denise said, which had us rolling. You can't tell her ass nothing okay.

We had the damn bus waiting 45 minutes on our slow asses. What could I say? Perfection took time. All six of us looked straight out of an urban men's magazine, each a different flavor of eye candy to fit your fancy. Guess they didn't know pretty bitches role in packs. Our cutie of a bus driver had a good time helping us onto our luxury transportation as he caught an eye full of these curves while we walked up the stairs one by one. I think he died and went to heaven when Denise came following behind after us because she had to stop at the front counter on our way out and had us head to the bus. My soror was hurting the game. Had the tatas sitting out with a hot pink fitted romper and those heels had her legs looking like they went on forever. That boy wanted to drink her bath water. That shit was right up her alley.

The club was packed, and it was jumping. Not only did Denise get a party bus, but we had full VIP access. We had a section and Bottle Girls came with the beverages as soon as we touched down. Endless drinks, so no waiting in line at the bar. Ha, what was a line? My glass stayed full all night, so I had no complaints. DJ Spindererella from Salt-N-Pepa was on the one's and two's and she had the crowd going.

"Shout out to all the lovely ladies of Psi Kappa Psiiiiiiiiiiiiiiiiiiiiiiii Incorporated in the building tonight. Make room so they can stroll," Spin said.

"Psiiiiiiiiiiiiiiiiiiiiiiiiiiiiiiiiiiiiiii Kapp," irrupted all over the room notifying everyone that Psi Kappa Psi was there. That intensified the party even more. Megan the Stallion's "Big ol Freak" was blaring through the speakers. Bri grabbed my hand and led us to the dance floor. My line sister was ready to act up and we were right along with her. Song after song, we showed our skills and we enjoyed every minute.

By 3:30 we decided to call it a night. My curls were sweated out, my edge control curled up on me, and my feet were hurting like hell but it was all worth it.

Time to head back to the hotel. We were headed back home tomorrow.

Chapter 19
Monica

That party was epic. Being high and drunk made it a little tough to keep my composure. Needless to say the struggle was real. Once we got off the bus, we started making our way through the casino to head up to the room. In the mist of this walk something caught my eye and stopped me dead in my tracks. I fell back from the girls to get a better eyeful. Justin was in a group of what looked like a wedding party. Ohhhhh maybe I could get some one last time before I left. Gone off that liquid courage, I tried to sashay my way over to him.

"Hey Justin. Looks like you guys have your own party going on over here," I said. You could literally see all of the blood rush from his face and he was as white as a ghost when he saw me.

"Let's cheers to the happy couple Brian and Tiffany!" one of the overzealous and very intoxicated wedding party shouted.

Then the bride in her veil and gown came over with a champagne filled flute in hand and laid a big kiss on her what seemed to be new husband, Justin. What the whole entire fuck? I had to shake my head back and forth cuz I know I wasn't seeing this shit right. The bride was white girl wasted so she totally missed that his eyes were locked on me the whole time in fear that I was about to blow his fucking world up in an instant. So Justin or Brian lied about his name, and that muthafucka came to Vegas to get married. The anger bubbled up through my veins and in a blink of an eye I slapped the shit out of him. My right hand left a red print on his face of fire for messing with the wrong one!

"You crazy bitch!" Justin/Brian yelled while he tried to lunge at me. Two guys dressed in matching tuxedos grabbed him before he jumped, and Denise and Bri drug me off to the elevator so we could get out of sight.

"You gone get us locked up in Vegas! What the fuck happened?" Bri yelled.

"Man, I don't care! He deserved it!" I yelled right back.

"Hold up everybody, stop yelling. Just calm down Monica and tell us what ol' boy did to you. Somebody text Krystal and tell her to get her ass back here ASAP." JaNae was trying to be the voice of reason in my chaos.

"He is a lying piece of shit. That's why I slapped him. I would have went Mayweather on his ass if y'all wouldn't have pulled me away," I said pacing the floor of the elevator until I heard the ding signifying that we made it to the floor that was selected.

The elevator doors swung open. Anger was spewing from my pores and at this point anybody could get it.

"Just a lying as bitch! Glad we are about to go home!" I said to no one particular. I just started packing my bags and slanging shit everywhere.

"You are too mad to deal with right now. When you are ready to actually talk, you know where we are. I can't deal with you acting like a damn child," Denise said as she left the room to leave me with my own BS.

In walked Krystal. What did they think she was gonna do? She supposed to be Captain Save A Hoe or somebody? I was not trying to hear her mouth either.

"I can hear all of you yelling outside the door. What's wrong?" Krystal asked.

"Girl, Monica got in a fight with some guy named Justin down in the casino, but that might not be his name. That's all of the tea I could piece together, sis," Daja added then shrugged her shoulders.

"First of all who is Justin? Is that why you got mysteriously sick at lunch?" Krystal shot at me.

"I wouldn't have even met Justin bitch ass if you wouldn't have cock blocked me with cutie with the green eyes I met at the bar," I yelled.

"You must be out of your fucking mind! Wayne is my man. We have been together for months. I didn't come out here chasing dick to cock block a damn thing, and wait a minute why is my stuff all over the room?" Now Krystal was fucking yelling at me too. These bitches were gonna stop yelling at me.

"Hold up. I know they not talking about our cousin Wayne bitch," Daja whispered to Bri.

"Girl yes. It's too damn much. Trust and believe I had some words with his ass," Bri replied.

"You're man! You didn't even tell me you had a man. You stay acting like yo shit don't stink because I like to have fun. You not better than everybody." I shoved her hard as hell out of anger because she was there. Tears began to fall.

"You not putting yo fucking hands on me. I don't give a shit what happened!" Krystal yelled. Then this bitch jumped dead on me. We fell on the bed and ex- changed blows, rolling onto the floor where we were entangled with our hands wrapped in each others hair. With my free hand I was trying to tag her ass as hard as I could with all my might. Fuck, I knew I was wrong. Krystal didn't do anything to me. I was mad at the world for not loving me.

"Aww shit! Where's the popcorn?!" Daja messy ass said while clutching her imaginary pearls.

"Stop it, stop it! Somebody help me break this shit up," JaNae insisted. It took three of them to break us apart.

"I don't know who hurt you, but it wasn't me! You're my sister. You were really going all in, trying to fight me like a bitch off the street. Look at my damn eye. I held back because I could have mopped yo ass! You always letting your drama with these nothing ass niggas get you out of pocket. The streets talk. Just cuz I don't say anything to you don't mean I don't know. You sleeping with this married one. Pregnant by that one. Getting passed around thinking you running some- thing. You just messing up your rep and your life!" Krystal blasted me in the front of everybody.

She was speaking nothing but the truth. The slit in my lip was a result of one of those sisterly hits she was referring to, but my actions hurt more than any number of punches we could have traded. What was I really doing? I was embarrassing myself and my organization. But for what? A bunch of assholes that don't give a damn about me. I sat on the bed and just cried. All of the hurt was pouring out of me from the horrible relationship I had with my father to the pain I felt from so many heartbreaks, continuously looking for love in all of the wrong places. Seeing yet another man use me and throw me to the side for someone else messed me up even though I initiated it. I just snapped.

"We not going out like this. We are sisters. Krystal stop for a second. Look at her. I know you see she is hurting," JaNae stated.

Even though I was dead ass wrong, my sisters embraced me. Each one of them wrapped their arms around me. Krystal cried with me and held me while I told them everything that I was carrying around on my heart. I'd never been able to talk to anyone about this. We all poured our hearts out about the shit that mattered. Bri was nervous about starting a family because she had guilt for giving up her first child for adoption. Denise loved a female that was pregnant with a child conceived with her stalker ass husband. JaNae was hella overwhelmed at home with more kids in the house and building her brand, which was growing by the minute. Daja was doing pretty good with her current situation so she was my she-roe.

"Sis, I know it's hard, but if you want to get professional help I have a wonderful therapist. Don't be afraid. If you need me to go with you, I'll pick you up and hold your hand the whole time until you feel comfortable," Denise told me.

Dela Morgan

Sisters cuss, fuss, and fight but at the end of the day we had each other's backs.

Chapter 20
Denise

Well, Vegas didn't owe me a damn thing. We had fun, saw a fight, and had healing. That was more like a sister 2 sister retreat if you asked me. I paid extra to have both of my bags in the overhead so I could avoid the hustle and bustle of baggage claim. Bri made us a Psi Kappa Psi Boule' playlist to send us on our way to end our trip. The selections went hard with songs we heard from the weekend and some of our favorite songs over the years. I was vibing so much I forgot to take my phone off of do not disturb until I got outside to wait on my Uber which had better be pulling up any minute. I had several missed text and a voicemail from Cherri.

"D, it's me. I know you're still out of town. I'm at my doctor's visit and they want to check me into the hospital immediately. I'm really scared. If it's not to much to ask can you please come to Texas Women's Hospital? I don't want to do this alone."

The message finished playing when my driver pulled up. I rerouted my destination so I could be there. I never wanted to admit it, but I loved Cherri. Afraid of being hurt, I concealed my feelings and lashed out with meaningless sexual encounters.

I tried Cherri's cell multiple times with no answer. My mind was running all over the place. God please don't let her go through the loss of losing her child as I did.

Once we pulled up to the entrance, I ran through the doors full speed in search for someone, anyone that could help me. I had to find her. The front desk gave me the directions to labor and delivery. Every second seemed so much longer. The elevator ride to floor eight seemed to last forever. I felt as though I couldn't breathe until the doors opened to let me out of the confined space and I could make sure she was okay. I ran to the nearest nurse's station.

"Can you please tell me what room number Cherri Anderson is in?" I asked the nurse asked in a full out panic.

"Are you a family member? There are only family members allowed," she replied.

"Yes, she is my cousin," I lied quickly on my feet. I was given the room number, and I made my way there. Before I went in I said another quick prayer for her and the baby to be okay.

When I opened the door, I saw Cherrie propped up in the bed feeding the baby. Oh my God she had the baby.

"I got here as fast as I could. I'm so sorry I wasn't here for you," I told her and kissed her on the forehead.

"It's not your fault, I'm just glad you're here now," Cherri said. She looked exhausted yet she had a beautiful glow of motherhood, which suited her.

"Would you like to hold her?" she said while smiling.

"If that's okay with you, I would. I'm sorry I didn't get you or the baby anything. I was in such a hurry, I'm so sorry," I tried to tell her.

"D, please stop. You just being here after everything is more than enough for me."

When she handed me the little girl a feeling of comfort and stability came over me. I didn't want to let her go, and I didn't understand why. I just loved her already. She opened her eyes and looked up at me and I saw why. This was the baby girl I saw in my dreams years ago when I was pregnant. I saw her face clear as day, a vision I would never forget. I just looked at her in amazement. One tear slid down my cheek. I could not believe what I was seeing. I was not ever leaving her side.

"What is her name?" I asked.

"Nothing I am coming up with fits to me, so I was going to see what you thought," Cherri told me.

"What do you think of calling her Jazmine?"

"After the flower?" she questioned.

"Actually, that's the name I had picked out if I was to have a girl."

"I love it, but whose last name is going to go first? Yours or mine?" she asked smiling. "I love you and I refuse to go any further without you. Jazmine is our baby, and I made sure of that on all documents. Say yes."

There was nothing for me to think about. This was what I wanted. All side pieces were now null and void.

Chapter 21
Brianna

My flight had just touched down in Houston, George Bush Intercontinental Airport. Getaways were nice, but it was good to be home. I must have forgot the drama that came with being surrounded by females for more than a day at a time. I loved em all, but I was ready to see my man. To top it all off the girls were fighting over some bullshit. I was sure they would work it out later. Reminiscing over the trip literally made me shake me head.

I followed the slew of people that I got off of the plane with as we all pretty much headed toward the same direction of the baggage claim. Getting to the carousel, I got a good spot to grab and go. While I waited, I texted my people and let them know I landed safely.

Chase: Perfect timing, I'm pulling up now.

That was Bae for ya! Alright, the noise alerted us that the bags were on the way so everyone had the eye of the tiger ready to fight for the death to get their belongings. The carousel started and multiple sized bags, luggage, containers, and even car seats were rolling on by. Out of the distance, I recognized my blue and white monogramed Kate Spade bag with the hot pink handles. I preferred to use colorful luggage and bags when I traveled, that way it was easy to spot from the hundreds of similar black bags.

Grabbing my overstuffed bag, I pulled the handle and prepare to roll it outside in that insanity we called Texas heat. When I walked out the door to passenger pickup within moments my eyes focused on my baby. That beautiful smile crept across his face and he headed my way. But did he have to look so delectable though in his white Polo and Blue shorts and white and blue Retro 13 Jordans? Good lord I was glad that was all me! That sexy thang approached me, grabbed me around my waist, and lifted me up for a much wanted welcome home embrace. He still made me weak in the knees and kept butterflies in my stomach.

"I missed you," Chase told me while releasing me to the ground where I had to catch my breath. My love took my bags and we headed to his truck.

"I see you coming out the house looking like a whole snack," I told him. Them dimples filled my heart as he smiled at my flirtation.

"Oh, I got a snack for you," he replied looking me up and down with a seductive eye. Best believe I knew what he meant, and we were damn sure on the same page. It was bout to be on and poppin when we got home. Popping the hatch, he put my things inside, and I headed to the passenger seat. Waiting on me was a dozen pink roses.

"Baby, thank you. You really did miss me," I told him once he opened the door to get in, and I proceeded to kiss him all over his face.

"Shouldn't be a shocker, girl I keep telling you that you are my heartbeat." Picking up my hand, Chase laced his fingers with mine and kissed the back of my hand. I was so happy to be home. For the duration of the ride home we caught up on what was going on while I was in Vegas. To me, this was what life was about. Just being here for one another, enjoying each others company. Bonnie and Clyde.

Somewhere in that almost 60 minute ride from the airport I drifted to sleep. Jet lag was a beast, I swear. Chase kissed me on the lips softly, awakening me from my cat nap, which notified me that we were home.

"Aww babe. I'm sorry I fell asleep on you."

"You know I'm not tripping love. I know you didn't get much sleep out there kicking it with your girls. You deserved to get away and have a good time."

"Well, now that I got a nap in I'm ready to make up for lost time, Mr. Reynolds." I needed to get a piece of all that hot sex on a platter. That crazy man pulled me by the hand and dragged me in that house so fast. I guess fuck them bags.

We both lost clothes much quicker than we put them on, showing that we were anxious to be intimate and yearned to be touched by one another. Picking me up Chase, inserted my favorite tool and being used do his body I naturally wrapped my legs around his waist. He roughly took me against the wall. My body replied to each and every stroke, wanting more and more and not letting up. Biting my lip, he kissed me dangerously. There was a time in marriage for making love, sex, and straight fucking. Fucking was what we both wanted and we both welcomed it. It wasn't cute and dainty or beautiful. It was passion and heat. Hair pulling, ass slapping aggression. Sliding down his frame, I wanted to give back. On my knees, I gripped his balls and took him into my mouth. Long and deep. Spitting and almost choking, I did my thang. Twisting with both hands that barely wrapped around him and sucking away, I noticed them toes curling while he gripped the counter behind him. Oh yeah, I had his ass going. Giving it my all, I took pleasure in his reaction to the heavenly service I was giving my well deserving husband. Ladies better take notice to pleasing their men, especially the good ones.

As if he couldn't take anymore, he pulled me up and bent me over the Italian marble counter top finish in his favorite position. Throwing it back, I gladly received all he was throwing in every motion. My body was talking to his, communicating the pleasure that we continued to give one another. Sweating, grunting, and moaning fills the kitchen air. Chase reached around me to find my clit to massage it. Damn it, he knew that drove me insane. I bucked, trying to get away from him and it was not happening. The pounding of his stroke stiffened, letting me know that he was close to his destination and the vigorous rotation on my clit was sending me in the same direction. The pounding got harder.

"Fuck me baby!" I yelled, and he did just that. Gripping my hips he pounded away. I surrendered to the threshold of my climax, which I had no control over and he followed behind shortly. Let's hope those little swimmers found a home. Panting heavily, we both were desperate to catch our breath.

"After that, I need something to eat. Girl you keep that up and I'm gone marry you again. Damn!"

"Boy, you are so silly. I don't ever want you to think I'm selfish in the bedroom. Once females get a ring a lot of them think they don't have to work just as hard to keep their man satisfied. Please let me know if I ever get tired so we can spice it up."

"Babe, you set the bar so damn high I can't wait to see where we go from here," Chase said kissing me.

We both were in need of nourishment after that "miss you" sex. Looking in the fridge, I saw that this man didn't cook a thing while I was gone. There were multiple to go containers stacked on top of each other. Shaking my head, I silently laughed. We made sandwiches and had chips and sodas to wash it down. I was not one for sodas too often but every now and then they hit the spot.

Once we finished our lunch, Chase took our dishes and started to wash them while I looked at the mail that came for me while I was out. A purple envelope stood out from the many white ones. Upon opening it, I saw that it was an invitation to what looked like a kids birthday party. That was odd.

As I read further, the invitation said that I was cordially invited to Ashley's 11th birthday party. There were more contents with the invitation that were pictures of my daughter Ashley Renee'. I covered my mouth and my eyes welled up with tears. There was also a note attached.

Dearest Brianna,

I hope this letter finds you in the best of spirits and good health. I am writing to invite you to Ashley's upcoming birthday party, which will be hosted at the club house near our home.

This is the time in her life that we all knew was coming. She wants to get to know her biological mother and find out more information on where she comes from.

You and I, as mothers to this beautiful girl, decided during our adoption process that if and when Ashley wanted to learn more about you the doors would be 100% open. We would love for you and your husband to come spend the weekend with us and enjoy the party. I hope to hear from you soon.

Shannon

I just sat there in the same place reading every word over and over, making sure I didn't miss one word.

"Babe, you okay over there?" Chase asked me. I couldn't even speak. I walked closer to him and handed him the contents of the purple envelope.

Connect with the Author

Facebook: D'Vine Pen

Instagram: @dvinepen

Twitter: @dvinepen

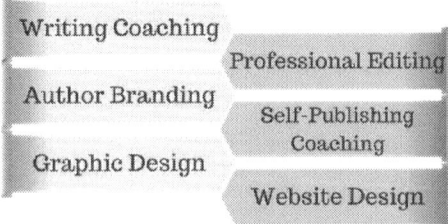

Creative Control With Self-Publishing

Divine Legacy Publishing provides authors with the guid-ance necessary to take creative control of their work through self-publishing. We provide:

Writing Coaching

Professional Editing

Author Branding

Self-Publishing Coaching

Graphic Design

Website Design

Let Divine Legacy Publishing help you master the business of self-publishing.

Made in the USA
Middletown, DE
01 September 2020

17061568R00102